As Her Name

Is So Is

Redbird

By Fay
Risner

Cover Art
By Fay Risner
All Rights Reserved

ISBN 10 0982459548
ISBN 13 978098245946

Booksbyfay Publisher
fayrisner@netins.net
http://www.writersownwords.com/booksbyfay

A list of the author's books

Amish fiction
Christmas Traditions

Nurse Hal Among The Amish series
A Promise Is A Promise
The Rainbow's End
Worldly Temptations

Amazing Gracie Historical Mystery Series
Neighbor Watchers
Specious Nephew
The County Seat Killer
Chance of a Sparrow
Moser Mansion's Ghosts
Locked Rock, Iowa's Hatchet Murders

Westerns
Stringbean Hooper Western series
The Dark Wind Howls Over Mary
Small Feet's Many Moon Journey

Ella Mayfield's Pawpaw Militia-A Civil War Saga in Vernon
County, Missouri

Non fiction

Alzheimer's books

Hello Alzheimer's Good Bye Dad-A Daughter's Journal
Open A Window-Alzheimer's Caregivers Handbook

To the woman he said, "I will make your pains in child bearing very severe. With painful labor you will give birth to children. Your desire will be for your husband, and he will rule over you."

Chapter 1

Hal Lapp took a deep breath and blurted out to her step daughter, "So, Emma, are you going to assist me with delivery when I go into labor?"

The iron skillet the sixteen year old girl had dried slid out of her hand and banged down on top the wood cookstove.

Hal flinched. "Mercy!"

Afraid to look over her shoulder at Emma, she turned the kettle she was washing toward the window for more light to see in it. She concentrated on the inside to see if she'd gotten it clean and continued causally, "It's just that I've been thinking. Right after our medical clinic was built, Jane Bontrager brought up the idea of using it for a birthing clinic. Since I haven't had one single Plain woman want to deliver here yet, it looks like I'm going to be the first. I need to plan for the big day. After all, I may only have two weeks left." Hal hesitated, thinking about what to say next. She had hinted at needing the girl's help before, but Emma always changed the subject. What would convince Emma to help her?

She looked out the window and saw evidence that her due date was getting closer. Mid March was showing hopeful signs of a much awaited early spring in Iowa. The sun basked the greening yard in a warm glow. Busy chickens scattered, scratching for an early nightcrawler or trying to uncover a nest of hiding lady bugs. One of Emma's roosters extended his neck and crowed several times. The other rooster answered from the barn yard.

Utter silence from Emma. Finally Hal twisted to look at her. The panic plastered on Emma's pale face highlighted her freckles. She was staring at Hal while she unconsciously wadded and unwadded the dish towel in her hands.

Hal insisted, "Well?"

Emma opened her mouth and closed it, struggling to find her voice. She took a deep breath and exclaimed adamantly, "Ach, nah. You can not be serious, asking me a question like that."

"Very serious. I don't have much time to waste. I have to have a plan in place. I'll need help." Hal pressed, "I want you to be my help."

Emma swallowed hard and stuttered, "I – I think we should pick a gute midwife to help this first time. We could both use some teaching about childbirth from someone with experience. I have never done such as this. You are a nurse and have taken classes, but you are the first to admit you have not the experience when it comes to delivering babies. For sure, you will not be a help to anyone assisting you once you are in labor. Another thing ----."

Hal interjected, "Why would you say something like I won't be a help?"

A blush flushed Emma's face as she pictured Hal in labor. She averted her eyes and busied herself scooting the skillet on the stove to a warmer place to finish drying it. "Believe me, it will all be very different from your view of things at the head of the bed. What if something went wrong? I would not know what to do. Another thing, I do not know how calm I can be when it is you I am helping give birth. We need someone else not related to you with experience enough to have a level head," Emma reasoned frankly.

Hal laughed. "You know what? I think you're right. We better come up with plan B before the end of March."

"Jah! And a whole team already in place very soon, just encase, to take care of the surprises," Emma predicted, rolling her eyes toward the ceiling. "As well as I know you, Hallie

Lapp, I know we need to be prepared for the unexpected. No matter what the situation, always when you are around we have surprises."

Hal giggled as she finished washing the last pan and placed it in the rinse water. She wrung out the dish cloth and proceeded to wash off the table. Emma dried the stainless steel pot and headed for the lower cupboard on the end of the counter. The pot hit the floor with a loud clatter. A gush of air expelled from the girl as she propelled back and braced herself against the counter.

Hal had been feeling edgy lately. It didn't take much to put her over the edge. She glanced from the pot on the floor to Emma and admonished, "Fudge! I didn't mean to upset you this much. I said I'd come up with a plan B. Why are you still upset?"

Emma shook her head. "That is not it. A mouse just came out of the cupboard and scared me."

Hal wrinkled her nose and searched the floor. "That's awful."

"Jah. Now we have to wash all the pots and pans it walked in," Emma said resignedly.

"That won't do a bit of good if we don't catch the mouse. He will be back in the cupboard in the night. Where did he go?"

Emma pointed behind the cookstove. "Under the corner of the wood box."

Hal studied the wood box with disgust. "We have to run that awful creature out from under there and get it out of the house."

"How?"

"I can have the boys bring in Buttercat," Hal suggested.

"You know Daed does not like a cat in the house," warned Emma, keeping her eye on the wood box for any quick movement of the mouse. "Is your memory so short you do not remember how Daed acted last time you brought Buttercat inside?"

Hal countered, "I remember all right that Buttercat is good at his job. Is your memory so short you don't remember Buttercat

3

caught that mouse."

Emma gave her a grumpy look.

"All right. We'll do this ourselves. We need to pull the wood box back, and the nasty animal will run out." Hal started for the opposite side of the cookstove.

"Stop!" Emma snapped. "You are not going to pull on that heavy wood box in your condition. I will do it, but what do we do to catch the mouse when he runs out?"

"Oh yeah." Hal thought for a second. "Give me a minute." She waddled out to the mud room and came back, holding the broom, handle first in front of her. "Now when I'm ready you move the wood box."

"You can not possibly think you are going to be fast enough to poke the mouse toward the mud room door and let him outside," Emma said dryly.

"That isn't what I had in mind," Hal huffed. She turned the broom around and stuck the broom's straw head over her shoulder. "Now I'm ready."

Emma took up position at the opposite end of the wood box. She waited while Hal sidled in the small space between the box and the cookstove.

"Now, Emma, tug."

Emma jerked. The box inched back. The mouse eased out and flattened to the floor, indecisive about what to do next. Hal lifted the broom and felt resistance as she swiftly brought the broom down. Even when she heard the grating crunch behind her, she kept the broom coming hard and fast toward the mouse. Not even the yelp from Emma kept her from her mission. That nasty creature wasn't going back in the pan cupboard ever again. Once the broom straws hit the floor over the mouse, Hal glanced over her shoulder. A dangling stove pipe, hooked to the wall pipe, quivered, spilling soot on top of Emma.

That dismal sight caused Hal to shift the broom slightly on the floor. She looked down as the mouse hunkered just beyond the broom then sprinted fast toward the cupboard. "Oh nah, the mouse is headed for the pots and pans again," Hal said in a panic.

She raised the broom over her shoulder, tangled with the pipe again. The blow put the pipe into a swinging motion. Soot sifted over Hal this time. Oblivious about the calamity behind her, she concentrated on her aim and clobbered the mouse. Once the broom was on top of the gross little creature, Hal quickly stepped on the straws. She watched the floor around her feet to make sure she had succeeded. A feeling of victory surged through her when she heard loud squeaks emitted from under the broom. Hal proudly announced, "I got him."

"You got me too," coughed Emma, batting at smoke billowing from the stove pipe attached to the cookstove.

Dumbfounded, Hal couldn't believe her eyes. Emma's face was streaked with soot and black specks continued on down her dress. Her white prayer cap was now mostly black and sifting soot into Emma's light brown hair. No way was that cap ever going to come clean. Maybe not even the dress. "Fudge! The pipe's broke. You're a mess," Hal stated.

Emma swiped with her dress sleeve at the black ring that circled her mouth to keep the soot from going into her mouth when she spoke. "You should not be one to cast stones. You are a mess, too," she wheezed disgustedly.

"Did I do all this?" Hal inquired disbelievingly, taking inventory of Emma, the mess behind the stove and the smoky room. Her throat began to tickle. She tried to wave the smoke away from her face with her hand but the effort was useless.

Emma retorted, "You certainly did. We better fix the pipe fast before Daed comes back. I am having trouble breathing with the way the kitchen is filling up with smoke," She reached for the dangling pipe and withdrew her hand quickly. "Ouch!" She snapped and put a finger in her mouth.

"What's wrong?"

"The stove pipe is too hot to hold, and it is bent. It will not fit back on the other piece without straightening the opening," said Emma, perplexed.

As if things weren't bad enough the living room banged. John called, "Hal, Emma, we have company." A pause then he said, "Hurry, Elton. The kitchen is full of smoke."

Bishop Elton Bontrager's voice filled with good humor as he replied, "Is Hal baking bread again?"

Hal rolled her eyes toward the ceiling. Why did John always tell Elton about her goofs so they could have a good laugh at her expense? Well, this was one time her husband wouldn't have to bother share with the bishop. Elton would get to see first hand, and she feared John wasn't going to find this dilemma one bit funny.

John, Elton and his wife, Jane, burst into the kitchen. Jane stared at Hal a second with her hand clamped over her mouth as she choked. The way her warm brown eyes sparkled, Hal figured the older woman was more choked from surpressing humor than on the smoke.

As John Lapp rushed across the kitchen, his dark brown eyes narrowed at Hal with annoyance. "Get the windows open." As he rushed behind the stove, he scolded, "Hal you should not try cleaning the flue out with a fire in the cookstove. This could have waited until spring."

Jane and Emma raised the windows. The breeze fluttered the white half curtains and thinned down the smoke in the room. Emma handed Jane a dish towel, and they moved about the room, waving their towels.

John took his chore gloves out of a hind pant pocket, put them on and grabbed the pipe hooked to the cookstove. He tried to fit it in the pipe sticking out of the flue.

Elton stood behind John, watching. His face changed from rosy red to beet red as he tried to breathe. "Can I help, John?"

Concentrating on his task, John said, "Somehow the stove pipe has gotten really bent. It will not slide together. Elton, get me a pair of pliers from the tool bucket in the mud room."

As the short, heavy set man rushed into the mud room, the back door slammed. Noah and Daniel past Elton and came into the kitchen. They stopped short and waved the smoke away

6

from their faces.

Daniel's doe like dark eyes widened as he whispered, "What is going on?"

"I do not think we better ask. Look how dirty Mama Hal and Emma are. From the way Daed looks, I think they are probably in trouble with him," Noah replied gravely.

"Why is it we always miss out when something gute happens?" Daniel groaned softly.

Hal held her breath as long as she could, breathed in and sucked smoke into her already burning lungs. She wrapped her arms around her expanding waist and coughed hard. Jane bolted around the table to help her and stubbed her toe on the broom handle. Hal caught the older woman as she stumbled. Jane uprighted herself, looked down to see what she tripped on and back at Hal. Her voice was a flat statement. "You are standing on your broom."

"I know," Hal said hoarsely.

Jane tugged on Hal's arm. "You must get out of here into fresh air. This smoke is not good for you to breathe."

"I can't leave yet. I'm standing on a mouse under the broom, and it may not be dead," Hal said stubbornly. "I don't want him to get away after we went to all this trouble to catch him."

From behind the stove, Elton said incredulously to John, "Did all this happen because of a mouse?"

"Sounds like it probably did," said John matter a factly.

"It would have been a lot simplier to bring a cat in to catch the mouse," Elton surmised.

"Here take the pliers," John said, ending the conversation.

Hal and Emma fanned their faces as they coughed. Jane held a hanky over her nose. "You both need out of here, mouse or no mouse."

"Wait!" Hal saw the boys, standing in the corner. She motioned to Noah and Daniel. "Come here." She said, "Daniel, place one of your feet between my feet." He did. "Now when I move my other foot you step onto the broom." Daniel gave Hal a thoroughly bewildered gaze as she stepped off. "You're standing on a mouse under the broom. I'll let you boys figure out how to get him from under your feet and out of the house. Please, after all this don't let him get away," Hal pleaded, patting her chest.

Once they got out on the front porch, the women inhaled deep breaths of fresh air between coughing spells.

When they quieted down, Jane exclaimed, "I can breathe so much better now."

"I agree," Hal said huskily, clearing her throat. The chilly east breeze picked up, causing her to shiver.

"You should have your coat on. This no time to catch a cold," Jane scolded.

"Nah, I don't want to have to wash the soot off my gute coat." Hal studied Emma a minute. "You look awful covered with black soot."

"You should see yourself. You look just as awful," Emma said and giggled.

Jane surveyed both of them and chuckled. Suddenly all three women were laughing until tears smudged the soot on Hal and Emma's faces.

Emma said, "I am going to get you a chair so you can sit down, Hallie. You have been on your feet long enough." She brought back two chairs, and a blanket for Hal. Jane opened the screen door to let her out. "Jane, you sit too and talk to Hallie. I'm going to get washed up and change clothes before it is time to fix dinner."

"Put on plenty of water and let me know when you're done with the tub," Hal told her.

After Emma left, Jane said, "Seems as though we picked a bad morning to come visit."

"I can't imagine what you think of me. I'm sorry you got in this mess," Hal declared.

"I am not one bit sorry. I can always count on you to perk up my day, Hallie Lapp," said Jane, giggling.

Hal looked over her shoulder and uttered ruefully, "Denki, but I hope John sees this morning that way. He's not so calm about accidents sometimes."

Jane chuckled. "In that case, we will leave as soon as Elton gets done helping John. We are on our way to Wickenburg. We stopped so I could find out if you have a plan in place for the big day. Are you going to the hospital?"

Hal's attention was on Noah and Daniel as they came from behind the house, headed to the barn. Daniel carried the mouse by its tail. The body looked limber. She didn't have to worry about Buttercat letting that one get away so it could find its way back to the house.

"Hal, did you hear me?"

Jane's voice brought Hal back to her company. "Sorry, I was watching the boys take the mouse to the barn and thinking good riddance. What did you say?"

"I asked if you had a plan for help when the baby arrives?"

"Oh, jah. It wouldn't be a very good recommendation if I went to the hospital and then expected Plain women to come to my birthing clinic when it's their turn. Emma didn't want me to be her first assist at helping a birthing patient so I'll ask Rachel Kitzmiller at church on Sunday to help me. Emma can watch and help her to get the experience."

"Des gute idea. I think you and Emma have made a wise decision. Rachel has brought many babies into the world safely. She is a gute choice," Jane said approvingly.

About a half hour later, John and Elton came out the screen door. Emma, scrubbed clean, was right behind them.

"We should leave," Elton told Jane.

"Denki for your help, Elton," John said.

"Hallie, I have your bath water ready," Emma told her.

"I'm glad. Come back soon you two." Hal waved good bye as the Bontragers walked toward their buggy.

John leaned against the porch post and folded his arms over his chest. "While you get cleaned up, Hal, maybe Emma could tell me what happened to turn the kitchen and the both of you into such a mess."

"Jah, Emma can tell you," Hal said quickly. She got a stern

look from Emma for leaving her to face John. As she let the screen door bang behind her, she said, "Be back when I'm clean."

In her bedroom, Hal pulled a purple dress from a peg on the wall. She opened a dresser drawer for underwear. Her hand hit a bottle that rolled out from under the stack of panties. Rose bath oil. She'd forgotten she smuggled that bottle in when she moved. Since Amish women didn't wear perfume, Hal was afraid that bath oil would be prohibited. With the mess she was in, this seemed like as good a time as any to transgress. She needed all the help she could get to smell human again. Besides, who would know besides her. She rolled her dress around the bottle and headed for the tub.

By the time Hal bathed and washed her curly copper red hair several times to get all the soot out, Emma had dinner ready. Hal made it to the table just in time. As soon as the family finished the silent prayer, Daniel wiggled his nose like a rabbit as he sniffed the air. "I smell something sweet, but it is not Emma's food." He sniffed again. "More like flowers."

Noah took in a deep breath. "Jah, I smell it, too. It is a pleasant smell all right. What can it be?"

Hal looked from one to the other boy, amazed that bath oil as old as hers was still so potent. She was already in more than enough trouble with John. She was dumb to add one more thing to her Make John Unhappy list. Why didn't she ever think of the consequences before she acted? Generations of dead Lapps were probably screaming protests from their graves about her offending transgression, smelling up their house with her Englischer bath oil.

Curious now, Emma sniffed and surmised, "It is the smell of roses. We do not have roses in bloom this time of year. Where can it be coming from?"

Hal ducked her head and picked at her food.

John leaned closer to Hal and sniffed. His lips twitched as he put her on the spot, "Hal, you are awful quiet, ain't? Have you noticed the sweet smell in the air?"

Hal gave John a painful I've been busted look. "I've noticed, hopefully, the smell will go away soon."

For the first time since John found the kitchen a mess, he smiled. He must have figured Hal had been through enough for one day. He winked at her as he said, "I think the boys will agree the smell of roses is much more pleasant than the smell of a kitchen full of smoke."

"Oh, jah," Noah agreed. "The smell is much better than smoke."

Hal relaxed and ate her lunch. Looked as though there was one advantage to being pregnant. Her family took sympathy on her for her mistakes.

Chapter 2

On Wednesday morning of the next week, Hal looked out the window at the dense, dark clouds. They obscured the hope of any sunshine. She turned loose of the curtain. It wasn't in her DNA to like dreary days. Her interest in outside perked back up when she heard wheels crunch in the rock as a buggy slowed down and turned off the road into the driveway.

"Emma," Hal called. "Samuel and Roseanna Nisely's buggy is coming in."

Roseanna lumbered down from the enclosed buggy. The very pregnant woman held her back as she stalked toward the house. Her wispy chestnut hair strayed from all sides of her prayer cap as if she had put it up in a hurry.

Her husband, Samuel's usually twinkling blue eyes looked worried. The children, Jimmy, twelve years old, and Ella, ten, their heads down as they walked behind their parents, were very subdued. Usually those two energetic kids raced to get to Noah and Daniel.

Hal jerked the clinic door open when Roseanna started up the porch steps with Samuel's help. "Was ist letz?"

"Es a vooderball gute thing that is the matter. You still plan to use the clinic for a birthing place?" Roseanna asked with a half smile, then she winched as she grabbed her bluging stomach.

"I certainly do." She looked past Roseanna. "Noah and Daniel are in the barn, kids. Go find them." As Jimmy and Etta took off, Hal ordered, "Samuel, help your wife. Bring her over to the bed and help her get seated." Once Roseanna was on the bed, Hal said, "Now, Samuel, scoot out of here. John's in the barn I think. This is women's work." Hal waited for Emma to come in and shut the door to the living room." Emma, we are delivering a baby." In nurse mode, she went to the table and grabbed the plastic sheet from the top of the stack of bedding they'd laid out for her own use. She turned back to Emma. "Put on water to boil and make sure we have plenty of supplies. Roseanna, wait a minute until I prepare the bed before you lie down. How far apart are the pains?"

Roseanna pushed a stray lock of hair off her sweaty brow as she thought. "Maybe ten minutes apart. Ahhh." Her face scrunched up in pain.

"I'd say you're going to be a mother again soon. The ride here may have helped you along," Hal said. "Now lie down." She put her arm behind Roseanna's shoulders and helped ease her on to the plastic sheet. Hal searched behind the stack of linen and came up with a small piece of folded flannel cloth. She offered it to Roseanna. "Want this bite into when the pains hit?"

Roseanna managed a giggle.

Hal looked at her in disbelief. "What's so funny? You know what's coming."

"I will not need to bite on cloth. My mother always says babies just pop right out of me like they did her. I will hold onto the top of the bed though to help with the pushing," Roseanna offered to appease Hal.

"I hope you're right about this. That means I've been blessed to have you as an easy first patient to help," Hal said.

Roseanna grabbed the top of the bed and grimaced when another contraction hit her.

Hal waited until the pain passed. "Let's see how far dilated you are." She suspected Roseanna couldn't be too far along as perky and calm as she was. What woman in her right mind giggled in the middle of painful contractions.

On further examination, Hal was astonished. She guessed wrong! Roseanna was nine centimeters.

"Is something wrong?" Roseanna asked, wiping with her blouse sleeve at the beads of sweat that popped up on her forehead.

"Not a thing except you will be a mother sooner than I thought. Very soon." Turning to Emma, Hal instructed, "Keep wiping Roseanna's face for her."

"I'm so excited. Samuel and the children can hardly wait to have a baby in the house," Roseanna babbled while Hal took her vitals. "Am I doing all right?"

"You're doing so well I'm jealous of how easy this is for you," Hal teased.

Instantly, Roseanna's quick smile left and a red flush covered her face. She got down to business with a hard push. There were several more hard pushes which Roseanna softly grunted her way through. Hal wondered if her stoic attitude was because she was Amish. Maybe this behavior was some Amish motherhood code that wouldn't allow a woman to loudly protest childbirth pain. The thought ran though Hal's mind she was pretty sure she wasn't Amish enough yet to silently suffer those sharp pains.

With Roseanna's next push, Hal was brought back to the moment. A baby boy popped into her hands as if he was in a real hurry to join the Nisely family. There weren't even any tears in Roseanna's perineum. Amazed at such a quick, uncomplicated birth, Hal decided Roseanna was right about one thing. Birthing was easy for her.

Hal gathered the baby in a blanket. "Roseanna, you have a boy." She handed the baby to his mother and turned to find a very unsettled girl behind her. "There you go, Emma. Your first baby delivery assist. You worried for nothing about helping, didn't you?"

14

Emma, gave a slightly doubtful nod. "Jah."

Hal said, "Bring the wash pans and warm water. You and me have some cleaning up to do. You can wash the baby, and I'll take care of the mother."

As soon as Roseanna and the baby were cleaned, and the baby was sucking, Hal asked, "Are you ready for me to call Samuel in?"

Roseanna gave her a tired smile and nodded.

Emma opened the clinic outside door to empty the pans of reddish water. She said, "Daed and Samuel are in the living room. I told Samuel he had a son."

"Gute," Roseanna said. "Samuel claims he can not pick a name until he sees the baby. Then he will know what name to pick."

"Maybe you can suggest a name to help him out," Hal commented, looking at the baby's fine blond hair sticking out of the blanket. "He's going to be the spitting image of Samuel I'd say."

"I think so, too, but it is up to Samuel to name our baby. That is the way it is done," Roseanna said.

Hal hadn't heard that little tidbit before. She already had names picked out for her baby. She hoped John gave her a chance to use at least one of them.

Hal opened the door to the living room. Samuel was standing right there, eagerly waiting to see his son. She smiled at him as he rushed past her.

So the couple could be alone with the new arrival, Hal said she'd go help Emma fix dinner. She stopped by John, in his rocker. "Mother and baby are doing fine." She felt a twinge, grimaced and rubbed her back"

John gave her a sharp inspection "That is gute, but how is Nurse Hal?"

"A little tired is all," she replied. After watching Roseanna give birth, she didn't want to complain about a minor twinge. "I better get in the kitchen and help Emma with dinner."

As she walked to the kitchen, Hal wished the nagging ache

in her back would ease up. It must be from her big stomach over balancing her these days. She was getting as sway backed as an old mare long past her prime.

Thank goodness for efficient Emma. While the girl heated water, she'd put on a large stainless steel kettle of vegetable soup. Enough for all of them.

Hal set the table and hunted up a box of crackers. That was all the energy she had. She sat down, feeling exhausted.

Emma called everyone to the table then she fixed a bowl, using a cookie sheet for a tray to take Roseanna.

After dinner, the men talked in the living room while Emma and Hal washed the dishes and cleaned up the kitchen.

Out of the corner of her eyes, Emma saw Hal make a face. "Hallie, are you all right?"

"Oh, just the usual aches and pains, a backache and a crampy stomach. I hate to complain about these little things now that I've seen how an Amish birth is done," Hal said with a slight smile. "My goodness, I wouldn't want to sound like a wimp."

Emma looked awe struck as she whispered, "I know what you mean. Do you suppose this is the way it is for all women?"

"Ach, nah. I'm pretty sure it can't be. Roseanna is just a super great birthing machine. That's all," Hal said in a hushed voice. "I should go check on her to see if she ate her dinner. I can bring back the tray to wash."

"Let me go get the tray while you sit down and visit with Roseanna," Emma insisted.

In the clinic, Hal checked out the tray beside Roseanna on the bed. The soup bowl was empty. She said, "Gute to see you have an appetite."

"Having a baby is work. Makes me hungry," Roseanna said and giggled.

Hal's smile changed to a frown. She grabbed her stomach as a stab of pain shot through her lower belly. "Oh my!"

Emma ordered, "Sit down quick, Hallie."

Hal started for the chair by the table but stopped. She felt a wet trickle run down her legs. She clutched her stomach and cried out. The trickle turned into a gush that made dark blotches on her blue skirt. Smelly amber liquid splattered on her sensible black oxfords and spread onto the floor.

"Oh, my goodness," Emma gasped, staring wide eyed at Hal's feet.

"Sit down, Hal," Roseanna said calmly. "Your water just broke. Now it is your turn to have a baby. Quickly, Emma, you need to help me up so you can remake this bed for Hal."

"Nah, Emma doesn't need to help you up," Hal protested. She grabbed her crampy stomach and gasped. "John can set up another bed for me. Emma, find Noah fast and tell him to head for the Kitzmiller farm right away." As the girl rushed outside and thudded down the porch steps, Hal groaned to Roseanna, "Why do babies pick such bad times to come?"

"Because they do not own a watch," suggested Roseanna, grinning. When Hal darted a that is not funny look at her, Roseanna said, "I am so glad I am here to see your baby born. I can not wait to greet your baby."

"I'm not so sure I want you watching after how easy you made it look. I'm afraid I won't hold a candle to the way you handled childbirth," Hal worried.

"Do whatever it takes. This is your first baby. Trust me, the first is the hardest," Roseanna said seriously.

Hal heaved herself off the chair and walked to the living room door. "John, we're going to need another bed in the clinic right away. Can you bring the one from the spare room down."

"Why?"

"You're going to be a father again. Very soon I hope," she stated. "Roseanna needs the clinic bed for a little longer so I need one of my own."

As the men headed to the stairs, Samuel slapped John on the back. "Now it is your turn."

Hal plopped down in the wooden chair to wait.

"Are they getting you a bed?" Roseanna asked.

"I'll have one soon." Hal answered with a dull grin. "You

know I think that's the fastest I've seen John move in a long time."

Emma brought in a pail of water and a rag. She got down on her knees and scrubbed the floor.

Hal said apologetically, "I feel like I should be doing that. I made the mess."

"Not on your life, Hallie. You get down here, and we would never be able to lift you up. We would have to leave you until the baby came," Emma scolded.

Banging and clanging came from upstairs as Samuel and John tore the bed apart. The men tromped down the stairs, carrying the parts. With a flurry, they put the bed back together and made two more trips to bring down the springs and mattress.

When they were done, John said to Hal, "Are you doing all right?"

"So far. You go keep Samuel company. Emma will come get you when the baby is here," said Hal, waving the men out the door.

Emma brought a fresh stack of linens and made the bed. As she helped Hal to lie down, another pain sliced from Hal's back to her belly, knotting her up in a ball. When the pain eased up, Hal snapped, "Ouch. That hurt!"

A burst of laughter came from Roseanna. She replied, "No kidding." Then she searched around her pillow and found the folded flannel material. She threw the piece onto Hal's bed. "Here you might need this."

Hal gave her a disdainful look, thinking, *"Whatever Roseanna does I can do. I have to as long as she watching me."*

Meanwhile, Daniel and Jimmy helped Noah corner one of the draft horses and get a bridle in his mouth. Noah threw his arm around the neck of the horse and hopped on with a speed that made the horse's ears perk up and swivel in alarm. Mama Hal was counting on him. He didn't have any time to waste.

Noah headed the horse toward the road. He lashed the hard stepping horse on both sides with the reins to get him moving fast.

Leaving a small trail of dust in his wake, Noah leaned into the horse and raced down the road. The familiar views on either side became a blur of green, blue and brown as he sailed by the barren fields, budding timbers, swollen creeks and greening pastures. Noah knew when he went by Elton and Jane Bontrager's house. He slowed the horse enough at the intersection to make the turn to head south. Before he knew it, he galloped past Luke Yoders farm. The Kitzmiller farm was just over the hill.

Luke's wife, Linda, was going in the house when she heard fast moving horse hooves. She stopped to watch as Noah raced down the road, disappearing in a second over the hill. She hurried inside. "Mama Margaret, where are you?"

Margaret thought Linda's voice sounded rushed. "In the kitchen," She replied as she came to the door. "Was ist letz?"

"Noah Lapp was going by here mighty fast just now. John does not approve of the boys running his work horses like that unless there is a good reason. Do you think it is Hal's time?"

Margaret thought a second. "From what I heard Sunday at church you could be right. Hal asked Rachel Kitzmiller to be her midwife." Her voice held concern. "Oh dear, Noah will not find the Kitzmillers at home. Their buggy went by earlier, headed for Wickenburg. I have not seen them returned yet. Not knowing she is needed, Rachel will not hurry to finish her shopping."

"Hal may need help now," lamented Linda. "Should we go see about her? We would be better than no help at all."

"Might be a gute idea. From what I heard of Hal and Rachel's conversation, Emma was very nervous about being alone with Hal when she went into labor and what not," Margaret said with a weak smile.

Linda ran for the barn. She hooked the horse to the enclosed buggy and pulled up by the house just as Noah sped back by. Linda would have flagged him down, but the boy went by too fast for her to get to the road. She called in the front door. "Better hurry, Mother Margaret. Noah just flew back by headed home with the bad news. Hal will be worried sick."

Noah was frantic. He didn't know what to do. Rachel Kitzmiller wasn't home. No way did he want to go back home without any help for Mama Hal. As he neared the Bontrager farm, he was struck by an idea. He slowed the horse down and veered into the yard. He hopped off the panting horse and tromped up the porch steps. Noah only had time to pound once on the door before Jane opened it.

She grabbed him by the arm. "Goodness sakes, Noah, come in. Something is wrong, ain't?"

"Jah. It is Mama Hal's time." He stopped to take a deep breath before he could continue. "She needs Rachel Kitzmiller, and Rachel is not home. I just have to bring a woman back to help Mama Hal. Can you come help?"

"Jah, I can. Go on home. I will be there as soon as I can." She closed the door and yelled, "Elton, hurry. Hitch up the horse to the buggy. It is Nurse Hal's time. I have to go to the Lapp farm quick. "

Noah straddled the tired horse and came to a sudden stop at the end of the driveway when he saw dust stirring up the air. He recognized the Yoder buggy. Linda and Margaret waved at him as they sped past. Noah knew what his hurry was, but he wondered about their hurry. He turned out on the road and heard the grate of wheels on rock. He looked back. Jane's buggy was already behind him and getting closer.

When Noah arrived home he was surprised to see the Yoder buggy by the house. He stopped at the barn and slid off the horse. Jane Bontrager pulled up behind the Yoder buggy and got down. Noah watched the three women greet each other and hurry to the clinic. He could quit worrying. Mama Hal had plenty of help.

Emma held the door as the three women filed in. Hal looked surprised see all of them.

Jane placed her coat on a wall peg. "Gute afternoon, Hal. You too, Roseanna. We did not expect to see you here."

"I have a new son. Came this morning," she replied. Tilting her bundle up, she pulled the blanket away from the baby's face.

Margaret and Linda stopped at the foot of Hal's bed. "Are you doing all right so far, Hal?" Margaret asked.

"So far," Hal hissed and groaned as she grabbed her stomach.

The women moved to Roseanna's bed and peered down at the baby. Linda asked, "What did Samuel name him?"

"Samuel James, but we will call him Sammy," Roseanna told them.

After a quick peek, Jane rolled up her sleeves as she approached Hal's bed. "We saw Noah go by fast and thought you might need our help."

"Noah should be back soon. He went to get Rachel Kitzmiller to be my midwife," Hal explained.

"Noah is back. He is putting the horse away," Linda said, patting Hal's hand.

"Oh, that's gute. Rachel will be here soon," Hal said, sounding relieved.

"About that," Margaret said slowly. "The Kitzmillers left home to shop in Wickenburg this morning. They are not home yet."

Sweat beads popped out on Hal's face. She said in a panic, "Rachel is supposed to be here. She said she would be."

"Now calm down. As long as she is not, you have us. We do know what to do since we have been through childbirth ourselves," Margaret assured her. She rolled up her sleeves, and Linda did the same.

Jane turned to Emma, "Is the water heating?"

"Jah, I think it is ready," she replied uncertainly.

Margaret asked in concern, "Do you feel all right? You look tired."

Emma fretted, "I did not expect to get so much experience at child birthing all in one day."

Margaret smiled and hugged Emma. "Hang in there, dear."

An hour later, Hal's contractions were closer together. Emma rubbed Hal's back. Feeling irritable about everything, Hal decided Roseanna was over doing her joyful cheerleading as she nursed her baby. She had to bite her lower lip to keep from saying so. Muffled footsteps paced in the living room. Hal suspected John was nervous. *Well, he should be. Her midwife was missing.* Samuel's low voice ramble on, keeping a conversation going to distract John.

"Is Elton in the living room, Jane?" Hal asked.

Jane patted her arm. "Nah, it is not our way to intrude on a family until after the baby is born. Margaret, Linda and me thought this was a special circumstance. You needed help."

A knock sounded on the door. Linda went to see who it was. "Rachel, it is gute you are here to take over," she greeted in a grateful tone as she let the elderly midwife in.

"With so many buggies here, I thought maybe I should stop and see if it is Hal's time," the wizen old woman rasped.

"It is," Linda replied quietly and pointed to Hal's bed with Margaret and Jane in attendance.

Rachel motioned her hand toward the other porch door as she said to her husband, "Joe, go visit with the men." She stopped to gaze at Roseanna. "It was your time, too?"

Roseanna giggled. "Nurse Hal delivered my baby this morning."

"Everything go all right?"

"Very gute, Rachel. I have a son," Roseanna said, beaming.

"Gute." Rachel turned around. "Now let me examined you, Nurse Hal." The midwife peeked under the cover then asked, "Has anyone put on water?"

Emma said, "Jah, I have water boiling for the clean up."

"Nah, I mean the tea kettle for a cup of tea. We might have a bit of a wait," Rachel said. "And shopping always makes me thirsty." She pulled a chair away from the table to the foot of the bed and sat down. "Now, Nurse Hal, stretch your feet out here to me. When you feel a contraction coming on let me know. I can control the pain."

"Like now," Hal said through clamped teeth, straightening her legs out.

Rachel took a foot in each hand and pressed her thumbs into pressure points in the soles. "Breathe deep in, Nurse Hal. Breathe out and keep that up. The pain will be gone quickly."

Emma hovered at the door long enough to watch Rachel so she'd know the procedure before she rushed past the men. They looked at her questioningly, and she shrugged her shoulders.

Her hands shook as she tried to fill the tea kettle. She spilled water all down the sides. When she placed the dripping kettle on the hot cookstove, dribbles of water did a hopping dance over the stove top. She stared at the kettle waiting for the water to heat and wished she could rush it. As soon as the kettle sizzled, she fixed the tea and carried a cookie sheet loaded with steaming cups to the clinic.

"What is going on in there?" John asked.

"We are having tea while we wait," Emma replied in a calmer tone than she felt.

As Emma disappeared, Samuel teased, "Tell the women they should tend to business. They can have a tea party later."

"Here is the tea, Rachel Kitzmiller," Emma announced.

"Gute, Emma." Rachel took a cup off the tray as she studied the girl. "You look peaked. Feeling all right."

"I already helped Mama Hal with Roseanna's birthing. I did not expect to have to help again so soon," Emma protested as she made the rounds with the tea.

"Stop looking like you are going to get a tooth pulled, girl. You are doing just fine, and you need all the practice you can get if you are going to do what I do some day," Rachel retorted, showing the girl no sympathy at all. "Take over for Jane, wiping your mama's face. Jane, the girl makes gute tea. Sit

23

down and have a cup."

Another hour passed before Rachel announced, "Keep up the good work, Nurse Hal. That baby is going to be born soon."

Loud knocks rapped on the outside door. "I did not hear anyone drive in," Margaret said. She answered the door and said bluntly, "Stella Strutt! What are you doing here?"

Stella ignored Margaret and didn't wait for an invitation to come in. She marched to the middle of the room, stood with her hands on her hips and confronted all the women lined up along the side of Hal's bed. "Saw the buggies. Saw all the buggies. Thought I might have missed that there was going to be a quilting bee. Maybe someone forgot to tell me. Accidentally forgot to tell me," she said testily as she looked from one to the other accusingly.

Hal groaned louder than before, and the groan didn't sound very painful. Everyone turned their attention to the mother to be. Jane smothered a giggle as she squeezed Hal's hand. She doubted Hal's outburst was contraction related.

Margaret explained calmly, "As you can see, Nurse Hal is having her baby. No quilting here today, Stella."

Stella's eyes darted from Hal to Roseanna. She took in all that was happening. "Maybe I can be of help," she offered sheepishly.

The women looked at each other and centered their attention on Jane, wordlessly imploring her to come up with something for Stella to do as far away from them as possible. Jane said, "Stella, how about you go see what you can find in the kitchen to fix for supper. We have a living room full of men and children that need fed."

"I'll be glad to do that – do that," Stella said. In a short amount of time, she was back. "Added some more vegetables to the kettle of soup on the stove. Should be enough. Should be plenty enough. Thought if I hurried I could get back in time to see the baby born."

Hal stuck her hands over her head and gripped the bed backboard. She gave a few hard pushes at Rachel's instructions.

The elderly woman held her hands between Hal's legs.

Suddenly, Hal relaxed, and Rachel straightened, holding the baby. "You have a girl, Hal." She tapped the baby on the bottom. The baby let out a kitten like cry. Rachel came around the bed and handed the baby to Hal. "You hold her just for a minute now. We have to wash her off. Stella, bring in two pans of water."

The women heard Stella Strutt's loud excited voice over the thud of her feet as she importantly announced to John and the other men, "Nurse Hal has a baby girl. A baby girl."

As soon as Hal was resting comfortably with the baby in her arms, the women sent John in as they made their way to the kitchen to finish getting the meal ready.

Not paying any attention to Samuel and Moses talking on the couch, Stella lingered outside the open door. Then she plopped down in the rocker as if she was taking a minute to rest.

"Are you all right, Stella?" Her husband, Moses, asked.

"Shhh!" Stella hissed as she cocked her ear toward the open door.

Hal held the blanket open. "Well, Daed, what do you think?"

"She looks like her mother. Look at that red hair," he said admiringly.

"What are you going to name her, John?" Roseanna asked.

"Looks like we have us a redbird. How about Redbird?" He looked at Hal for agreement.

Hal said timidly, "We should really give her a more appropriate name. How about naming her Cardinal Emma Lapp and calling her Redbird."

"I think that would be just fine," John agreed. He placed a finger on top the baby's soft red hair and said proudly, "Wilkum to the Lapp family little Redbird."

Tromping heavy footed to the kitchen as fast as her swollen feet could carry her, Stella, with a sad expression on her face, clucked her tongue. When the women continued to work on supper, she said in a hushed voice, "I feel sorry for that poor little baby! Poor little baby."

25

The women turned to stare at her. Jane said softly, "Stella, what is wrong with you? Why pick on that baby? It just got came into the world. It is just fine. Roseanna and Samuel have a healthy boy."

"Not the Nisely baby. I am talking about the Lapp baby. Poor Lapp baby," Stella lamented.

Linda Yoder looked toward the mud room door, fearing Emma might show up any minute from gathering eggs. "This is no place to say these words. That little baby is pleasing to look at and healthy."

"She might be, but you saw all that red hair. She is the image of her mother. Just like her mother," Stella lamented, shaking her head from side to side.

Very puzzled by Stella's concern, Rachel said, "I have caught many girl babies. From what I have seen, they usually look like their mothers."

"That is unfortunate for this baby. Unfortunate baby indeed," Stella repeated, clucking her tongue loudly. "All that woman's wild blood is in that baby. You can see it. That little girl does not stand a chance. You mark my words. Mark my words."

"I do not want to hear another word of this nonsense from you, Stella Strutt. Help me set the table so we can eat. Noah and Daniel will be in from milking soon, and our men need to get home to chore," Jane said coolly.

Stella didn't move. She hissed, "If her red hair and the look of her mother is not enough to convince you of her wild blood, maybe what John named her will be." Again the women lined up to listen, curious this time. Stella pointed toward the clinic and said in disgust, "They are going to call her Redbird. How awful is that?"

Margaret said thoughtfully, "Redbird. I like that name."

Jane agreed, "It is an original name and fits her red hair. John did gute." She noted with satisfaction Stella's defeated look. "Now we need to get the food on the table, Stella. No more dawdling."

Chapter 3

Early April brought on warm days. Hal did what she could to help Emma as her strength came back. They spring cleaned the house from top to bottom. Hal piled the rag rugs on the front porch. While Emma swept and mopped the floors, Hal shook all the rugs. She liked that job, because she didn't have to pay any attention to what she was doing. When she picked up the first rug, robins hopped about the yard, looking for a nightcrawler. They flew off when the rug snapped. Purple martins, carrying dried hay and grass nesting material, flew over the house, headed for their complexes mounted to a high pole in the back yard. A flock of honking geese, coming from the north, verged low behind the barn and landed in the pond.

Hal had helped Emma washed the windows on the inside and now they waited for a warmer day to get the ladder out and wash the outsides. With a good dose of spring fever, Emma laid off rows in the fall plowed garden under tautly stretched string. She planted radishes, lettuce, spinach and potatoes, hoping a late freeze didn't come along and bite off the tender plants.

While Emma worked in the garden, Hal raked the leaves off the flower bed at the end of the front porch and broke the soil up so that the sprouted tulips and jonquils would have an easier time growing. When she had time, she'd be in the back yard, hoeing tender grass out of the rhubarb, asparagas and winter onion beds.

School let out in mid April. One morning, Noah and Daniel started cleaning the barn right after breakfast. About an hour later, the boys plunged out the barn door, calling for Hal and Emma as they raced to the house. Each boy wanted to be the first to deliver some kind of news. Noah made it through the door first, and Daniel slammed the door behind them, waking Redbird up.

They collided with Hal at the kitchen door on her way to pick up the crying baby out of the cradle near the heating stove. "Do I get two guesses as to which one of you slammed the door and woke baby?"

Daniel hung his head. "I am sorry. I forgot."

Hal said dryly, "Looks like I only need one guess. What was your hurry?"

"We wanted you to come see the new chicks in the barn," Noah said excitedly. "Daniel just found them."

Emma joined them. "We have chicks this early? Where was the hen sitting?"

Noah shrugged his shoulders. "We do not know. We just found them in a pen."

Hal stopped rocking the cradle, and Redbird didn't complain. She whispered, "Let me put on my shawl, and I'll go with you. I want to see the chicks." She stared down her nose at Daniel. "But only if we can go quietly out the door so we don't wake the baby again."

"Jah," the boy said contritely. "I will be more quite."

Emma said, "I want to go, too."

The boys led the way between the barn pens. Noah pointed. "Here she is."

At the sound of his voice, the red hen stopped scratching in the straw bedding and clucked loudly. Her two tiny yellow chicks tumbled over the straw to get to her. She sat down on them and fluffed up so she looked twice as big as she was.

"Is two chicks all she hatched?" Emma asked,

disappointedly.

"Jah, two is all we found," Noah replied.

Daniel opened the door and walked into the pen. "We want to look at the chicks again," he said to the hen.

At his approach, the hen bristled up and said angrily, "Arragh."

"Careful, Daniel," Hal warned. "That hen doesn't want to be disturbed. We'll see them again some other time. Better leave her alone."

A few days later, early on the day promised to be a pleasant one. After breakfast, Emma went to feed the hens. She'd put four loaves of bread in to bake to take to the church meeting on Sunday.

The kitchen always smells wonderful when Emma bakes bread, Hal thought as she took on the task of washing the kerosene lamps. She had the kitchen table covered with lamp parts. She'd washed the blackened glass chimneys. That was a weekly job she was always glad to be done with. Her fingernails always needed a good cleaning afterwards to get the soot out from under them. She was refilling the last lamp with kerosene when John came in from chores with a suggestion. "How would you women like to go to the Wickenburg salebarn with me and the boys?"

Hal stuck a sparkling clean glass chimney on each lamp base as she listened. "I'd love to go. I'm tired of being cooped up in the house doing house work." She glanced hopefully at Emma who had just come in the mud room door. The girl looked doubtful. "Emma, please come with us. Whatever needs doing will be here another day. Besides, I want to see if I can find you that rooster I owe you."

"You do not have to do that," said Emma, with a wry smile. "But I agree it would be nice to get away from home."

As the Lapp's enclosed buggy rolled along the road, Hal took a deep breath of fresh, crisp air. She bask in the early morning sun that shone through the buggy windshield, warming her as she listened to the children chatter behind her. They were excited about this excursion. It seemed going to the salebarn was a big adventure to them.

The countryside was such a burst of color this time of year after an all brown and white winter. The red clay road was bordered by green grass and wild flowers peeking through laid over dried grass from last summer. Red and yellow tulips and purple and white hyacinths dressed up farm house flower beds. Yellow budded spirea and lilac bushes scattered about yards added to the look of spring. Chilled ponds were covered with wild ducks, resting before they headed north. Creeks wound along the base of hills, covered with misty, surreal fog that concealed the water which had not yet warmed up.

John caught up with a possession of buggies headed for the salebarn. On the south edge of Wickenburg, he followed the other buggies into the salebarn parking lot and skirted behind pickups and various size stock trailers. He crossed the dusty gravel lot, headed for the long hitching rack that bordered a line of evergreen trees and drove behind the parked enclosed buggies and carriages. Hal smiled when she read the humor in one man's hand painted sign on the back of his buggy. "Energy efficient vehicle: runs on oats and grass. Caution: Do not step in exhaust."

John pulled in an empty parking space at the end of the line. He climbed out and tied the horse to the hitching rack while his family unloaded. They walked toward the salebarn with other Amish families.

Redbird woke up when the cool breeze hit her. She squealed. Hal put the blanket over her face and snuggled her close, patting her back until they entered the salebarn. Sounds of various animals in the back and tantalizing smells of food coming from the cafe met them at the door.

The sprawling building jumped with action under the bright lights. English farmers and Amish ones gathered in small knots, talking and laughing. John stopped to talk to a couple of men. Noah and Daniel headed for a group of boys.

Emma said, "Hallie, let's pick a spot to sit."

Horseshoe shaped wooden seats tiered down to the arena in front of the auctioneer stand. Above the stand was a stuffed longhorn bull's head. He made a good mascot, but looked old enough to have been in some of John Wayne's westerns when he was still alive.

Noah and Daniel joined them on seats below Hal and Emma. John seated himself beside Emma. Once the sale started selling sheep all eyes were on the ring. It didn't take long for Daniel to grow restless. He twisted and fidgeted to check out what the rest of the crowd was doing. Next, he elbowed his brother and got a hissed, "Stop that." Daniel grinned as he tugged on the bottom of Noah's denim jacket and waited for Noah's reaction. Noah glared at him and pushed Daniel's hand away.

Finally, John had enough of Daniel's teasing his brother. He leaned forward and put his hand firmly on his young son's shoulder. Daniel stilled instantly. John whispered sternly in his ear, "Stop rutsching around. Leave your bruder alone. You are here to watch the sale." Daniel turned contrite as he put his hands in his lap and watched the ring.

A tall, heavy set sheep buyer took bids on his cell phone. Hal remembered it used to be when she went with her dad to the salebarn buyers had to be in the salebarn seats so the auctioneer could see them motion with a finger or hold up their number card. Now the buyers called their bids in, and someone else did the bidding for them.

The sheep buyer flipped the flap shut on his phone as a dozen fat lambs ran from the ring, then answered it again. He stood up fast. Faster than Hal would have thought a large overweight man could have moved. The sheep buyer searched the walkway over the top of the seats and found the person he was looking for. A tall, thin man, in a faded gray flannel shirt and worn blue trousers, staggered out of the cafe. He put his hand against the wall to steady himself. Behind him but back several feet was a watchful teenage boy wearing worn clothes. The sheep buyer sprang up the steps and grabbed the bearded man's arm in a tight grip. The man's red face glowered even

31

brighter at the sheep buyer. "You turn loose of me," he shouted, trying to shake the buyer's grip off his arm.

The auctioneer stopped taking bids, because all eyes had turned to the walkway. The sheep buyer kept walking as he tugged the bearded troublemaker along with him. "I will turn loose when you get to the door."

The auctioneer took charge of his prospective buyers again. "No need to pay that man any mind, folks. He's leaving." He looked at the weigh scale and noted the weight had registered for the sheep behind the wide door. He nodded at the man in the ring to open the door. "We got to keep moving if we want to get this sale over with today so let in the next lot of sheep."

Hal whispered, "Emma, why is that sheep buyer being rough with the Amish man?"

Emma glanced in the direction Hal nodded. "That man is not one of us," she hissed. "What did he do?"

"I didn't see him do anything. He came from the cafe, and the sheepbuyer grabbed him," Hal told her.

"Did not pay for what he ordered maybe. That has happened with him before," Emma said matter of factly.

"He looks like he's been drinking," Hal surmised.

"That does not surprise me," Emma replied cryptically, turning her attention back to the ring.

Hal touched Emma's arm and nodded again. "That boy seems to be following them. Looks enough like the man to be his son."

"He is," Emma hissed with a disgusted glance at the boy about her age. "Nothing but trouble from that one. Just like his father."

By that time, the two men arrived at the steps down to the outside door. The boy leaned against the wall, folded his arms and pretended to watch the ring. The sheep buyer gave the drunk a push down the stairs. He said roughly, "Don't come back."

The man held onto the railing to regain his balance and lumbered down the few remaining steps. Hal could only see his head and shoulders at the bottom of the steps as he paused. Thinking that his warning was clear, the buyer returned back down the steps between the seats to his spot in front of the ring. Slowly, the drunk turned and looked up to make sure the sheep buyer wasn't still watching him. He nodded to the boy to follow him, turned and walked through a side door.

Hal watched the boy come away from the wall. With slow, deliberate steps, he followed. She elbowed Emma. "Where does that door go at the foot of the steps?"

"One goes outside and the other to the small animal and poultry auction room." Emma looked above the auctioneer's desk at the clock. "We might as well go there now. It starts in a few minutes, and you clearly are not watching the sheep sale," Emma teased as she stood up.

Not as many people were in the small auction area, and most of the spectators were women. Hal and Emma stopped at the door when they saw the bearded man. He was standing by the edge of the ring, waving his hands around excitedly as he talked to two Amish men.

Near the door was the unkempt boy leaning against the wall, looking around him with a surly expression. His clothes were faded and threadbare to the point one of his grimy knees showed from a tear in his slacks. His brown farmer shoes had seen better days. Unconsciously, he raised his right hand and scratched himself under his sweaty left arm. The dirty fingernails on his blunt fingers were long and chipped. Hal could smell his body odor. When was the last time that boy had a bath? She felt sorry for the poor boy and wondered what the rest of his family was like now that she'd seen his father.

Suddenly, the troublemaker's voice held a blustering sound as he towered over the two Amish men. They frowned their disapproval at him, but they didn't speak back. One of them whispered something in the ear of the other, and they moved away to go to the seats. The drunk grabbed the nearest man's arm and boomed, "You must listen to me."

Redbird squirmed at the loud voice. There were two helpers

in the ring carrying clipboards, a man and a woman. The man perked up at the sound of the angry voice. He laid his clipboard down next to stacks of egg cartons and slipped his cell phone from his denim jacket pocket. With her ear tuned to the ring man, Hal looked into noisy cardboard boxes of fuzzy yellow and black chicks, ducklings and goslings, all in a row on the tables. The man said softly into the phone that he needed help to evict a fellow causing trouble. Before Hal and Emma reached the end of the tables, the menacing sheep buyer towered over the bearded man in a face off. After a few choice words, the buyer again led the man to the outside door and gave him a shove. This time he took a wide stance in the door with his burly arms folded over his chest and watched while the man walked behind the parked stock trailers. The troublemaker turned once to see the buyer hadn't budge. "Keep on going," shouted the sheep buyer. The troublemaker did what he was told that time. As soon as the sheep buyer left the area, the boy moseyed to the outside door and trotted across the pavement to catch up to his father.

Now that the excitement was over, Hal took time to check out all the other items for sale. She couldn't get over the variety. On two tables were baked goods, breads and pies, along side stacked cartons of fresh eggs. At the end of the tables were rhubarb and raspberry plants in dirt filled coffee cans. They walked along a row of small wire rabbit cages. In larger wire cages, geese protested confinement loudly, and several cages held half a dozen laying hens or a rooster or two.

Eight small wooden pens contained newborn lambs and tiny kid goats. Hal reached down and patted a lamb on the head. It immediately moved its head, lashed out with its tongue and nibbled at her fingers. "He likes me. Isn't he cute?"

Emma snorted. "Cute, jah, but work. He would nibble anyone's hand, because he wants a bottle of milk." Afraid Hal would lose her head and bid on the lamb, Emma took her arm and led her away. "We can not buy everything that is for sale here. Let us see what all the barking is about in the next pen."

A litter of Jack Russell puppies, a mix of colors, white, brown and black, yipped all at the same time. Emma said, "They must be fresh weaned and missing their mother. They would be glad to nibble on your hand, too."

"I'll take my chances," Hal said as she leaned over the wooden pen and patted the two puppies that jumped up and down to greet her. Hal held Redbird over the pen so she could see the puppies. "Aren't they sweet, baby?"

Emma gave Hal a curious look. "Hallie, do you miss having a dog?"

"Oh, maybe sometimes, but I think the boys miss a dog more," Hal admitted. As she looked around, she said, "I'm so glad we came. This has been so much fun, seeing all this. It's almost like going to a zoo. Now do you see one of these roosters you like?"

"Hallie, you do not have to get me a new rooster. I forgave you a long time ago," Emma teased.

"I know that, but I want to," Hal insisted.

Emma moved back down the line of cages. She stopped at the end cage as the rooster stretched his neck and crowed. "All right then how about this young one."

"Are you sure? He sounds like he has a sore throat?"

"He is vocal enough to enjoy, and his crow will deepen as he ages. He is young enough to be useful for awhile," Emma assessed. "Maybe even just young enough that the other roosters will not pick on him."

Hal studied the red and black rooster and agreed. "He's very pretty. I can't wait to see what you name him."

One of the cardboard boxes in the row on the tables caught Hal's attention. The box emitted a din of cheeping above all the other boxes. Hal peeked in again. "How about we get this box of chicks to give the hen in the barn. She only has two babies. She could use a larger family."

"That is not necessary. She did not have a good hatch, because it was too cold. Some of the hens will have better hatches later on. We will have plenty of fryers to butcher,"

Emma assured her.

"I know, but these chicks will grow fast and be ready to butcher before the others are. The hen will take care of them, won't she?"

"Jah, if we put them under her at night she will," Emma admitted.

They made a trip to the office to get a bidding number and took their seats just as the auction began. When the bidding started on the box of chicks, Hal bid until she got the box. Then they waited until the bidding got to the rooster. Hal won him, too. Now she felt better about being the cause of Emma's pet rooster's untimely death.

At noon, the Lapp family met at the cafe door. If looking used made a difference, this cafe must have been very successful over the years. It was no secret that Amish women were among the best cooks. Perhaps it was because they cooked the old fashion way from scratch with what they had on hand. From the moment the Lapp family went through the door, they smelled the different dishes cooking and knew they would like whatever they ordered.

Faded red leather, six person booths lined one wall. Above the booths were large black and white pictures of the salebarn arena, taken thirty or forty years ago, with the ring full of black calves during a fat cattle sale, Hampshire hogs or fat lambs.

A large glass case near the kitchen was filled with a variety of fruit and cream pies; rhubarb/strawberry, cherry, apple, banana, coconut, and vanilla cream with thick meringue. Hal read the menu board above the case and wanted to order the coconut cream pie. Below the list of pies was scrolled by a wise Amish cook, "It's my theory if you look confident you can pull off anything even if you don't know what you doing."

A small freezer was next to the pie counter. Written across the front side of the freezer with a black marker was, "Friendship is not such a big thing. It's all the little things that count."

A shelf above the freezer held cigarette packs and rolls of

chewing tobacco. No doubt the cigarettes were bought here that scared up the Formica tables back in the days when smoking was allowed. Most of the booths were filled with farmers or families as were the stools at the counter. All the talk floating around centered on an agriculture theme; the price of calves, livestock feed, crops and high gas prices.

The Lapp family read the dinner menu board. They found it hard to decide if they wanted the whole meal or a sandwich. A young Amish woman, in a pale green dress, greeted them with a pleasing smile as she centered her pencil over the pad, ready to take their orders. Each of them made a choice between the pork steak dinner or a baked pork loin sandwich and French fries.

Hal ordered the loin sandwich and the coconut pie.

The waitress said, "Sorry, the coconut pie is gone."

Hal studied the pie list. "I've never had peanut butter cream pie. I guess I can try that."

As they ate, Hal said to Emma, "It's fun to eat out once in awhile instead of doing the cooking, ain't?"

Emma nodded as she took a bite of her pork loin sandwich.

Hal found she liked her peanut butter pie very much and looked it over carefully to see if she could make a pie like it.

The waitress came back for a stack of dirty dishes. She smiled at Hal. "How did you like the pie?"

Hal replied, "Let's put it this way. I'm glad you were out of coconut pie."

That brought giggles from the waitress and the Lapp family.

After lunch, John picked up Hal's purchases. He set the box and cage in the back of the buggy with the kids. Next he drove them to the Amish grocery store. Several of the other salebarn goers must have had the same idea. The middle of the parking lot held several cars, and the outside edge was lined with buggies. John and the boys waited in the buggy for Hal and Emma to do the shopping.

Emma stopped at the display of garden seed. "We should buy more seed before it is all picked over."

"Why are the packets brown?" Hal asked, looking at the rows of different wooden pockets with only a name on the front of each pocket and printed on the packets.

"The seed is bought in bulk and packaged here to sell. They do not get fancy by putting pictures of the vegetable on the front," Emma said, picking out several packets.

"Wait a minute!" Hal said. "That packet says Deer Tongue on it."

"Jah."

"I can't imagine growing a deer's tongue, and even if you can, I don't think I could eat it," Hal said, being very sincere.

Emma looked at the package then grinned at Hal. "It is not what you think it is. This is a kind of head lettuce."

Hal let out a gust of air. "Oh, thank goodness."

On the way home, Hal pondered about the farmer that caused the trouble in the salebarn. She asked John about him. John frowned as he answered. "His family does not live far from us. They are not Plain though they let Englischers think they are. They get by with more meanness that way, but make it bad for our Plain Community." As if that was should be enough of an explanation, John twisted to look behind him. "Daniel, Jimmy Klopfenstein was full of riddles again today. Heard one you might like."

"Tell us," Daniel said eagerly.

"Do you know how long cows should be milked?"

Daniel thought a minute and asked, "Noah, how long do you think?"

"Expect the same amount of time it takes to milk each of ours, but I do not know exactly how long that is," Noah reasoned.

Daniel gave up. "Nah, Daed. How long?"

"It takes as long to milk a long cow as it does a short one," said John, grinning.

The boys and Emma chuckled heartedly. After that the only chatter in the buggy came from the box of chicks and the young rooster that sound like he had a sore throat.

Chapter 4

It was just about time for the evening milking when the Lapps pulled into their driveway. The Holstein cows were banked up at the milking parlor door, bawling that they were ready.

A buggy was parked by the house. John pulled around it and parked. Emma told the boys to each take a sack of groceries to the kitchen. She picked up the box of chicks and handed her father the rooster cage.

Hal pulled the blanket tighter around Redbird before she stepped down. Bobby Keim, a slender, dark haired young man, came to meet her in the driveway. He never failed to give everyone a level gaze from dark eyes that never seem to smile. He had shouldered the responsibility as man of the house at a young age when his father died, and he took the job seriously.

"Gute afternoon, Bobby," Hal greeted. She knew the Keim family from visiting with Bobby and his mother, Lovina, on church Sundays. She liked the family and hated it that she hadn't been able to get Bobby's younger brother, Adam, to warm up to her, but she kept trying. He seemed smart enough though from birth he hadn't been able to talk. Understandably, that made him self conscious and shy around others.

Emma walked up beside Hal, carrying the cheeping

cardboard box. "Hello, Bobby Keim. Been waiting long?"

The young man gripped the brim of his black hat and twisted it around in his hands. "Gute afternoon, Emma. Nah, not long. What you got there?"

Emma opened the box top so Bobby could peek in. "Baby chicks. We went to the salebarn today."

"Kind of early for chicks as cool as it is yet, ain't?"

"We had a hen steal her nest out and hatch two chicks. We thought to put these under her to enlarge her brood," Emma told him.

Bobby stuck his finger in and poked one large chick. "This turkey, too?"

"What turkey?" Hal asked, coming closer.

Emma stared at the brown fluff ball. "That is a turkey all right. I did not see him among the chicks before."

"Me, either, but then I wouldn't know what I was looking for," Hal said, smiling. "Will the hen take a baby turkey?"

Emma nodded. "Sure. She will not know the difference if we put the chicks under her in the dark tonight." She looked up at Bobby, "Did you want something?"

"Jah, my mother is sick. I wanted to know if Nurse Hal could come look at her." He answered Emma as he looked at Hal.

"Sure I will. Emma, I'll put Redbird in her cradle. She shouldn't be hungry again until I get back. Wait for me to come back so I can help put the chicks under the hen. Bobby, I don't know where you live so I'll follow you with our buggy as soon as I put the baby down and get my nursing bag."

Hal was familiar with the way as far as the Kitzmiller farm. The rest of the way, she memorized landmarks as Ben clip clopped behind the Keim buggy. One farm they past had several houses and many outbuildings at the back end of a long driveway. Three men and several teenage boys were in a field next to the road, planting corn. The men stopped working and stared curiously at the buggies going by. Hal thought one of the men was vaguely familiar, but she couldn't place where she'd seen him. An instinctive feeling warned her to be glad she wasn't any closer to him.

Farther down the road, Hal looked back at the pinched together farm buildings and the narrowness of the field with tiny figures working in it. She chided herself that it was her over active imagination at work again. There had been no reason for her to be uneasy.

When she reached the Keim farm, Bobby parked by the barn. Hal stopped in front of the house and went to the door, not waiting for Bobby to catch up. Adam opened the door before she could knock. He nodded at her. "Gute afternoon, Adam. Bobby says your mother isn't well. Show me where she is, and I'll see if I can help her."

Adam nodded and beckoned with his hand for her to follow to his mother's bedroom.

"So you're in bed, Lovina," Hal said, sitting down easily on the edge of the bed. Her keen eyes picked up a much too frail, middle aged woman who appeared to have been ailing for some time. Surprised by the woman's appearance, Hal tried to recall the last time she'd seen Lovina at church.

"Afraid so," Lovina said softly, pushing her prayer cap in place over her graying hair as she sat up. "Adam, put on the coffee pot so Nurse Hal can have a cup. She is probably chilled from her journey and will have a cool ride home. Close the door as you leave."

"What is the matter?" Hal asked.

"Ist letz is I am as weak as a newborn calf." Lovina's voice sounded strained.

Hal asked, "How long have you been this way?" She studied the elderly woman's round sun wrinkled, very pale, gaunt face that hadn't seen sunlight lately.

"About three weeks. Could not even go to church," Lovina lamented.

That explained why Hal hadn't seen the change in Lovina before. She patted Lovina's hand as she commiserated, "Neither could I. I just had a baby in March."

41

Lovina brightened up. "That is voonderball gute news. You should tell me about the baby. Boy or girl? John and the children must be so happy."

"They are. It's a girl."

"What did John name her?" Hal had the feeling Lovina was avoiding the subject of her health. "Her name is Cardinal Emma, but we call her Redbird because she has lots of bright red hair. Now we should get back to you. I take it from the weight loss you haven't been eating much."

Lovina picked at the quilt to avoid Hal's eyes. "Nah, but I just do not have an appetite."

"Any pain?" Hal asked.

"Nah. Well, none to speak of," Lovina said lamely.

Hal gave the woman a sharp look. "This slight pain not worth speaking about, where is it?"

Lovina rubbed her mid section. "Around my stomach."

Hal took Lovina's vitals. As she rolled up the blood pressure cuff to it put away, she said, "Your blood pressure is higher than it should be. That happens sometimes when a person doesn't feel well." She took Lovina's hand and pinched her forearm lightly to check dehydration.

At a tap on the door, Hal called over her shoulder, "Come in."

Adam entered with Bobby behind him. Adam handed a steaming cup of coffee to Hal. He offered the other to his mother. She said, "Not now." He nodded and put the cup on a small chest by her bed and watched Hal sip from her cup.

"This is delicious," Hal declared. "Adam, you are a gute coffee making. This hits the spot. Denki.

Adam gave her a shy smile.

Hal felt victorious. *Chalk one up for me. I got him to smile.* "Adam, maybe I should watch you make coffee sometime. I'm terrible at it. After the one time I tried, Emma won't let me near the coffee pot again."

Lovina and Bobby laughed. Adam's smile grew wider.

Bobby winked at Hal. "Not much chance my bruder would

let you watch him make coffee. He will not even let his own mother and bruder watch him to see how he does it."

"This is the truth," Lovina said as she slipped down in bed.

Watching his mother, Bobby got to the point. "How is our mother?"

"Frankly, I don't know what's wrong with her. You need to take her to the doctor. She's losing weight and not drinking enough liquids. She's dehydrated which makes her feel worse. Lovina, you should try to drink as much liquid as you can. Coffee isn't the best to drink. Water would be better." Hal met Bobby's gaze. "It's no gute feeling ill all the time when she could get better with help from a doctor. If you'd like I can take her in my car. It would be an easier and faster ride than in your buggy."

Bobby darted a look at Adam. Adam raised a questioning eyebrow.

Hal saw the doubtful looks. "Remember it's all right for me to use the car when it is a medical problem. Let me know if you need me." She eased off the bed. "Now I need to get home to my baby."

It was a densely dark night by the time Bobby walked out with Hal to the buggy. He held a lantern high to light her path. "Smells like rain. Do you want me to take you home? Adam can follow with our buggy."

"Nah, you shouldn't both leave your mother. I can manage. Ben surely knows his way home by now. I trust him," Hal said and chuckled. She patted the horse's rump and dodged Ben's swishing tail before she climbed into the buggy.

Hal snapped the reins lightly over the horse's back to get him moving and slowly turned the buggy around. Once back on the road, she leaned forward to peek out the windshield at the sky. No stars and no moon. The sky was one big black cloud. Bobby might be right about it raining soon. The headlights didn't help her see very far into the murky blackness in front of the horse. She hoped she'd been right to place her faith in Ben finding his way home. She'd like to be home before the storm started.

Small lights glowed off to the side of the road in the distance. The way the lights bobbed Hal thought it must be a few early lightning bugs. When she was even with the lights she realized the glows were larger.

A pack of dogs darted from the ditch and barked ferociously at the buggy wheels, filling Hal with alarm. The horse shied sideways, startled by the attack. "Easy, Ben. Easy," Hal called, holding the reins tight to keep him from taking off.

Out of the darkness, two forms, with lanterns swung high in the air, closed in on her. A couple more stayed back behind the first two. In front of the buggy, a harsh voice yelled, "Get out of here, dogs." The sharp command caused the horse to flinch and step sideways. The dark form grabbed the harness near the horse's head and commanded him to whoa. The horse backed a step and stepped forward, rocking the buggy back and forth.

Feeling as jittery as Ben, Hal pulled back on the reins, fearing he was going to run away. "Whoa, Ben. Whoa." When the horse settled down, she snapped loudly, "Get away from my horse. You're scaring him." *Me, too, she thought.*

Two of the men with the bobbing lanterns stopped beside her buggy. Trying to keep a quiver out of her voice, Hal demanded, "What do you want?"

The man, by Ben's head, walked beside the horse and stuck his face next to the buggy window. He was an older man with a gray beard that widened as it lengthened. In a harsh voice he demanded to know, "Are you Nurse Hal?"

"I am."

"My wife is hurt. You will see to her." His voice had a ring of authority that left Hal no choice but to obey as he pointed at the driveway.

"All right. Back away from my buggy so I can pull in," Hal said reluctantly.

One man on each side with lanterns held high to light the way and two in back, they escorted her as the elderly man led them. He reached for Ben's harness and called whoa in front of a large two story house. A curtain fluttered in the lit upstairs bedroom window. Hal was reminded of when Emma used to peek out at her.

Hal climbed down, wondering what was going to happen next. The elderly man demanded curtly, "Follow me."

It was too dark to make out much about her surroundings, but the large house in front of her looked to be in bad shape and in need of a coat of paint. She looked behind her. Two men and two teenage boys were beside the buggy, holding their lanterns high.

Once she entered it took a few seconds for her eyes to adjust to the lighted room, dimly lit at best with weaned light from dirty kerosene lamps.

A gray haired, Amish dressed woman, in a rocker by the heating stove, was alone. She rested her head back and didn't move although her face registered surprise when she saw Hal.

Assuming she must be the patient, Hal picked a kerosene lamp up off a small table near the door. She noted it was next to a half full bottle of cheap whiskey and kept going. Hal set the lamp on the floor beside the rocker. "Gute evening. I'm Nurse Hal. Your husband says you aren't feeling well. Can you tell me what is the matter?"

The woman darted a glance at her then averted her faded brown eyes that were as worn as the dress and apron she had on. She looked over Hal's shoulder at her husband. Clearly, she was puzzled by the appearance of a nurse. Hal twisted to see the elderly man practically breathing down her neck. The other two men were by the door, leaning against the wall and still holding the lanterns. One, a burley sort with a grim face, had a half smoked cigarette sticking from his lips. Both men had on dirty clothes that were stained. The room wreaked of sweat and unbathed bodies.

As Hal studied the other man she remembered where she'd seen him. The tall, slim built man was the troublemaker kicked out of the salebarn that morning. Her face must have gave away that she recognized him. Though he couldn't be sure where they had met, he could tell from her face that she didn't have any use for him. His lips curled in a sneer as he eyed her with a bald insinuating expression that made her skin crawl. She tried to appear calm, but she didn't feel that way at all closed up in the room with these three rough looking men with questionable repetitions.

Hal ordered the older man. "Bring me a chair to sit on."

He stared at her, freezing her with his cool assessment. He wasn't used to be spoken to in the same tone he'd used on her. His voice was even colder when he ordered, "Henry, bring Nurse Hal a chair."

The burley man, with bristly black whiskers, carried a wooden chair from the back corner to her. He looked her up and down like he was evaluating livestock. Hal eyed him unflappably right back until he lowered his eyes and backed away. She focused on the old man. "I see no need for any of you to stay around. I'm not used to caring for a woman patient with so many men breathing down my neck. I'm sure your wife will feel easier if you leave."

That didn't go over well. The old man's piercing eyes reminded her of a hawk, keenly watching for the moment he might choose to attack, not approving of and suspicious of her every move. He folded his arms over his chest and stayed put.

Hal eased into the chair and set her bag on the floor. From behind the couch, a mangy, black lab, with ribs showing, slinked out and crept up to Hal. He must have thought she had food in the bag, or he hoped she did. He sniffed it. She moved too fast to rescue her bag from his germs. The dog stiffened and let out a deep angry rumble through bared teeth. Hal slowly put her hands in her lap and snapped, "As you men leave, take this dog with you. I don't relish getting bit for my trouble."

"Take the dog and go on home," barked the old man. "Leave one of the lanterns here for me."

The door behind Hal opened and shut. She hadn't won completely but two out of three men gone was a good thing.

"Now what is your name?" She inquired of the woman.

The woman licked her dry lips and elongated slowly in a nervous voice, "Nonnie."

Taking note of an oozing cut centered in a large bruise on her right cheek bone and a split in her upper lip, Hal asked, "Nonnie, how can I help you?"

"My wrist hurts so much I can not use my hand." She spoke painfully slow as she nodded to her hands in her lap. Hal wondered if that was Nonnie's nature. Or, did her words come slowly because she tried to make sure she said the right thing to please her husband? With a grimace, she lifted her right hand off her left wrist.

Hal felt of the swollen, black and blue wrist. When she pushed in, Nonnie let out a sharp cry. The woman's snaggled teeth, with intermittent gaps, reminded Hal of a picket fence in bad need of repair. Teeth like that couldn't be good for the woman's health. "Nonnie, I'm so sorry I hurt you. Your wrist is broken. You need it taped up and in a sling for about a month or six weeks to rest it while it mends. You really should go to the doctor and let him see if the break in the bone is in place so your arm mends correctly."

Nonnie didn't speak. Her face was expressionless as she looked over Hal's shoulder.

Hal dug around in her bag and came out with a roll of wide gauze. She wound a thick layer around the broken wrist for support.

The door behind the rocker squeaked open. A girl about Emma's age, round faced with a slim nose and wide set dark brown eyes, slipped quietly into the room.

Hal smiled at her. "Hello, what's your name?"

The timid girl looked at the floor as she said softly, "Annie."

"I'm Nurse Hal. My step daughter is Emma Lapp. You know her?"

Annie darted a glance at the older man and back at her feet. "Nah."

Hal lowered Nonnie's arm back into her lap. "Annie, do you

think you can bring me a piece of material?"

The girl looked puzzled.

"An old sheet or something like that for me to make a sling with to hold Nonnie's broken arm up," explained Hal.

Annie nodded and rushed back the way she came. Hal sat back in her chair. "How did you come to break your arm, Nonnie?"

The woman said flatly, "I fell."

"You should be more careful. I can tell that was a bad *fall* you took," Hal said with meaning as she looked Nonnie in the eyes. "Put a cold wash cloth on your cheek every so often. That will help with the bruising and swelling. Keep that cut clean so it doesn't get infected. I'll put some butterfly stitches over it. When the strips curl up and fall off, the cut should be mended enough that it will stay shut." Hal brought a packet of smaller butterfly stitches out of her bag and applied them.

The old man started pacing back and forth behind Hal, keeping her nerves on edge. Finally, he snapped, "What the devil is taking that girl so long?"

Nonnie excused meekly, "Annie had to hunt for the right material to use. She will be here soon."

Just then Annie appeared, holding out a piece of sheet. "Will this do?"

"About time you showed back up," the old man snapped, glowering at her.

Annie curled into herself like a frightened, abused deer in a hunter's gun sights.

Hal held her hand out, and Annie edged forward to hand her the material. "Denki, this will do fine," Hal said. She tied two ends in a knot and folded the piece then gently placed Nonnie's arm in it and pulled the knotted end up. "Duck your head so I can put the sling over it. Now how's that."

"Gute," Nonnie said.

"You won't be able to use that arm for awhile. Are you right or left handed?"

"Right handed," Nonnie replied.

"That will help. You use your right hand for most things like washing up and eating. Just rest the left arm and wait for your wrist to heal. I know you're in pain. If you have aspirin take one about ever four hours. It will help some," Hal instructed, patting Nonnie on the knee. She stood and faced the old man with a level gaze, "I've done all I can. I'm going home now."

The old man picked up the lantern and held the porch door open. "I will walk to your buggy with you. I would not want you to take *a bad fall like my wife.*"

That sounded like an ominous warning to Hal, but she didn't know for sure why he felt as if he had to threaten her. She feared she had spoken too sharply or pried too much to suit the old man. He was smart enough to realize she didn't believe his wife injured herself in a fall.

Hal climbed into the buggy and shut the door. She hoped she was going to be able to leave without something happening to her. The man took hold of Ben's harness and guided him around so Hal was headed down the driveway. She looked behind her at the glow of the lantern. The distrustful, old man watched a minute to make sure she kept going before he headed toward the house.

As Hal drove by a chicken house, a feeble yellow light filtered through the fly speckled, dust filmed window. Just for an instant, a bearded man appeared then ducked from sight. There was enough glow out the glass for Hal to see the door was barred from the outside. The man was locked in.

As Ben clopped his way home, apprehension nagged at Hal. Every shadow on the road cast by a tree gave her a catch in her breath. She strained to see if faces of those men was leering at her from the darkness. She felt as if Ben was trotting in slow motion, taking forever to get her home where she'd be safe. She hated not being able to see her surroundings in the dark.

All sorts of what ifs popped into her head as she strained to see out the windshield. What if a deer jumped out of the ditch and scared the horse? What if Ben didn't know the way home and took a wrong turn along the way? What if those men

49

weren't through with her yet? She had talked rudely to them. Maybe she made them mad enough to come after her. After all, the old man hinted at a threat to harm her.

The peck of rain drops splatting softly against the windshield brought Hal back to reality. Soon the drops turned into a downpour, making vision worse yet which added to her gloom and doom attitude.

Chapter 5

Ben slowed on his own and turned into the Lapp driveway. He headed over by the barn. Hal called whoa, grateful to be home safe and sound. She rushed toward the house as Noah and Daniel came running to meet her in the driveway. Noah shouted over the pouring din, "We will take care of the buggy and Ben."

"Denki," said Hal as she kept on sloshing through the puddles.

She'd almost made it to the porch when Noah stopped her. "Mama Hal, there's something in the buggy?"

"What?" Hal called.

"Do not know yet. It sounds like a cat. Did you pick up a cat at Keims?" Noah shouted to be heard over the rain.

"Not that I know about," Hal called. Curious, she raced back through the pouring rain to the buggy. When she got to the buggy she could hear the mewing sounds. "There sure is something in there. Daniel, bring the lantern from the barn so we can look."

Daniel was back in a second. Noah took the lantern from him and stepped up into the buggy. He said in consternation, "Ach, nah! It is not a cat."

Hopping up and down to see over Hal and Noah, Daniel

asked, "What is it?"

Sounding mystified, Noah said, "A baby."

"It can't be." Hal pushed Daniel out of her way and rushed inside. "Oh my! It is a baby. Poor little thing." She picked up the wiggling bundle and felt dampness on the bottom side of the blanket. "I've got to get this baby in where it's warm." She held the protesting baby close and bent over to protect it from the driving rain as she headed for the house.

Once inside, like a wet dog, Hal shook her head to shed water from her thick hair.

John glanced up from his bible. "About time you got home. We were worried." At the sound of his loud voice, the baby developed a stronger cry. "What have you got there?" He asked, dropping his bible in his lap.

"A baby," Hal replied as she patted the infant, trying to soothe it.

Instantly, Emma was off the couch and in front of Hal. "Why? Whose?"

"I don't know, but hold the poor little thing while I get out of this wet coat. It's really raining right now," Hal said, giving Emma the baby.

"This baby is wet," Emma said. "No wonder it is unhappy."

"That and it's cold and hungry." Hal shrugged out of her coat, held it out the door to shake the excess water off and placed it on a peg next to the other coats. "Come with me while I examine this not so joyful bundle," she said as she headed to the clinic. "I haven't a clue what is going on. Noah heard the baby crying in the buggy and thought it was a cat, but it wasn't. I was just as surprised as the boys when I found this baby had been stowed in my buggy."

Emma shook her head in dismay as she and John followed Hal. "Who would leave a baby in your buggy?

"I don't know. Lay the baby on the table, Emma," Hal said

"No reason to be a baby at the Keim farm." John hesitated a second. "Is there? I guess Lovina Keim has been poorly and missed church Sundays for some time."

"John Lapp, what an awful thought! She's too old to have a baby. Lovina is poorly but not from having this baby. The Keim farm wasn't my only visit. I was on my way home when five men stopped me on the road. The older man's wife broke her wrist and needed my help. I was at that place for a while, but I didn't hear a baby while I was there." Hal opened the blanket. "This baby is only a day or two old. No one even bothered to wash it properly. Emma, bring a diaper and some warm water." Hal took the dirty diaper off which was a small flour sack dish towel and wrapped the baby back in the blanket. "The baby is a girl. I'll feed her so she quiets down."

Hal took the straight pins out of her blouse front as John persisted, "Hal, finish your story. You say some men stopped you?"

"Jah. When I drove by in the daylight, I saw some men and boys planting corn in a field in front of several houses and a lot of outbuildings. I think that may have been the farm where they stopped me. I thought at the time there must be a very large family living there," said Hal, sitting down by the table. "It was so dark by the time I came back along I really wasn't sure where I was at when the men came at me."

John said grimly, "You shouldn't have stopped at that farm. If you have to see about Lovina Keim again, tell Bobby he is to ride with you both ways. Those men are rough. The Plain community does not like their ways. They like Englischers to think they are Plain, but they do not follow the Ordnung. They are not wilkcum in our community."

When Emma placed the pan of water and a diaper on the table, Hal laid the unhappy baby back down and removed the blanket. "I can believe that. John, would it have hurt you to tell me more about them when I asked this afternoon. I'd have been prepared for meeting them," she scolded. "Not that I had any choice. They made me go with them to the house. I did recognize one of the men. He was the one that caused all that trouble in the salebarn this morning."

"That was Henry Hosteller," John offered.

"The teenage boy that followed that man around in the salebarn was with them on the road, but he didn't come in the house," Hal recalled.

Emma supplied, "That was Henry's son Marvin."

"The other man was heavy set with bushy black whiskers."

"That would be Eli, Joseph's other son," John said. "Now tell us what happened."

"Like I said those men didn't give me a choice. They came out on the road and stopped Ben. I was ordered by the older man to go take care of his wife, because she needed help. He took hold of Ben and escorted me off the road to the house. He certainly gave all the orders."

John said, "That was Joseph Hosteller. What was wrong with his wife?"

The baby squalled as Emma washed her. "Hush little one. I will be done soon," soothed the girl.

Hal continued, "She had a broken wrist. She said she fell, but it was plain she'd been beaten. She was afraid to say much with three men standing behind me. Truthfully, that was probably why they were in the room. So that poor woman wouldn't talk to me. I finally ordered all of them to leave."

"You ordered them to leave?" John looked at her like she had lost ever bit of her good sense. "Talking like that to those men when you were alone could have been dangerous."

Hal nodded agreement as she concentrated on the baby. Emma had finished washing her. "I found that out. Nonnie's husband didn't much care for me ordering them around, but he made the two men leave. He wouldn't go no matter how hard I looked at him. So I couldn't ask Nonnie to tell me what really happened. As scared as she was, she probably wouldn't have talked anyway."

"What are we going to do with this baby?" Emma asked, picking up the pan of water she'd dumped the wash cloth and the make shift diaper in.

"Care for her for now," Hal answered. As Emma started to leave, she asked, "Oh, is Redbird all right?"

"She was missing you earlier, but I fed her the bottle you left," Emma said.

"It was for times like these that I prepared that bottle so Redbird wouldn't get off schedule or too upset. I don't know what I'd do without you, Emma." Hal bent over the baby. "Look at this. We need to clean and disinfect the cord. It's tied off with a piece of binding twine. Whatever the mother cut the twine with, she used the same knife or scissors to cut the cord afterward. See the fibers on the end of the cord. Good way to get bacteria into the baby's system." Hal sighed. "What a terrible night for this baby and me."

"This baby was abandoned. We need to tell the sheriff about this and let him hunt down the mother," John declared.

"Give me a few days to make sure she's going to be all right. The sheriff won't do anything about finding the mother. We'd have to give her up to foster care. Technically according to an Iowa law, I'm a Safe Haven since I run a medical clinic and that includes my buggy or car. Newborn babies can be left for me to find or handed over to me with no questions asked," Hal reasoned. "I'd like to care for this little one for a few days just until we're sure the mother won't have a change of heart."

After Hal finished feeding the baby, the infant went to sleep, and Hal laid her down in the cradle with Redbird.

Emma said, "Now while the two babies are quiet you better eat. I kept you a plate of supper in the warming oven."

"Denki, I'm suddenly very hungry." Hal said when Emma placed a full plate in front of her. A few sleepy cheeps from behind the stove drew her attention. "Oh, nah. I forgot about the chicks. We still have to take them to the hen. I'll eat fast."

It was still raining when Hal and Emma slipped into their coats. Hal carried a flashlight and Emma the chick box. Emma stopped Hal at the barn door. She said softly, "When we get in the barn shine the flashlight very low to our feet. We can not startle the hen, or she will fly away."

They edged along between the row of pens, looking in each for a sleeping hen hunkered down in the straw bedding. Emma spotted the hen toward the back of the last pen. "Hallie, there she is. See her in the far corner. Turn the flashlight off. We will move up to her slowly."

In the darkness, they eased through the dry straw and cringed at each rustling step for fear the hen would wake up before they were close to her. Emma squatted and set the box down. Hal hunkered beside her. Emma reached into the box and took out a chick. She set the sleeping baby down and pushed it under the hen's left wing. The hen let out a croaky groan to protest being bothered, but she didn't move.

"I want to put a chick under her," Hal whispered, sticking her hand in the dark box. She eased the tiny soft body under the hen's other wing. The hen wiggled as if shifting her weight from one foot to the other and settled back down.

Hal and Emma put the chicks under the hen one by one. Disturbed by being moved from the box, the chicks woke up enough to know they had found a different warm, dark place to sleep. One that smelled like home. The cheeping chicks pushed each other around, trying to move farther under the hen. That aroused Mama hen enough that she stood up and checked to see what was wrong with them. She scooted some of the chicks farther under her and sat back down, screeching softly in her version of humming to quiet her babies.

Emma stood up, picked up the box and walked quietly out of the pen with Hal behind her. Hal turned on the flashlight so they could see their way out of the dark barn. They dashed into the pouring rain and headed for the house. Hal called to Emma in front of her, "That was fun."

The next morning, John was up with the first burr-ring of the alarm clock. He dressed and woke the boys. There was much to be done in the fields, but if the soil was too wet, they could work on machinery and with the livestock. Emma hurried downstairs to fix breakfast. Hal dressed and fed a fussy Redbird and her new cradle mate. Once the babies had full tummies they fell back asleep, Hal moved cradle downstairs to the end of the kitchen table.

"What have we got planned for this morning, Emma?"

"Looks like the sun is going to shine. We need to wash clothes. You can hang them on the line while I make a batch of cheese. Maybe you can make butter in between hanging clothes," said the organized girl. "By the time we have that done, we'll fix dinner. Daed and the boys will be eager to get back to their work."

Later, Hal decided she had done pretty well with her share of the chore list Emma gave her. By mid morning, she'd churned the butter. She bent over and took the last pair of John's pants out of the basket. She penned the pants to the line. Now the wash was done. She stopped to lift her bare feet one at a time and shake off water from the wet grass as she watched Bobby Keim drive in. He was in a hurry as he across the yard to meet her.

Hal took a clothes pin out of her mouth and dropped it back in the clothes bag before she could greet him. "Gute morning, Bobby. Is your mother feeling worse?"

"Nah, this is about something else. Come to the buggy with me." When they reached the open door, Bobby said solemnly, "I need you to go inside."

Puzzled, Hal followed Bobby up the steps. He scooted across the seat out of her way. "Look in back."

As battered as the teenage girl was Hal couldn't say for sure if she knew her. "Is it Annie Hosteller?"

Bobby nodded.

The girl was stretched out on one of the side seats in back. Her head stuck out from under the cover. When she heard Hal's voice, she raised her head with an effort and squinted through very frightened, swollen, blacken eyes. A gash in the middle of a bruise on her left cheek was dripping blood to her chin. Clearly, she had been badly beaten. "Help me get her into the clinic, Bobby."

They managed to get the girl as far as the edge of the bed before Annie's knees weakened enough that she collapsed. Hal grabbed her by the shoulders. "Bobby, get her legs and help me lay her down." By the time Hal took her arm from under Annie's shoulders the girl was breathing heavily from the exertion. She put her arm over her eyes to block the light.

"Just relax, Annie." Hal said. She pulled Bobby over by the door and said in a hushed voice, "That girl's clothes are damp. She was out in the rain. Tell me what happened."

"She ran away from home in the middle of that downpour last night. She was soaking wet when she knocked on our door. Could barely walk in her condition. She asked me to hide her so I let her in. Mama gave her a nightgown to sleep in and stretched her clothes out close to the fire so they dried some. In the light of day, she looked so bad I thought she needed to come see you. She did not have any other clothes to put on but what she was wearing."

"I can't go back home," Annie cried as she choked on a sob. "Papa's buggy passed by us as we came here. They are looking for me. I might not survive the next beating I will get for running away."

Hal and Bobby rushed to her. Bobby knelt beside the bed. He took Annie's hand, and his concern for the girl was obvious. "You're safe here. Nurse Hal will take gute care of you."

"You can stay with us, Annie. We aren't going to send you home ever," Hal vowed. She took Bobby aside again and said in a hushed voice, "Bobby, you did the right thing. By the way, I met the Hostellers last night and Annie. Her mother needed my help. I have a very clear and scary picture of what those men are like. I saw how they had beat Nonnie Hosteller."

Bobby looked appalled.

"John was upset that I'd been at the Hosteller farm. He said if your mother needs anymore help you should come get me and see that I get home safely. Last night those men didn't give me a choice. They pulled me off the road and escorted me to the house. I wasn't so sure I was going to be allowed to go home once I saw what Nonnie's injuries were."

"I am sorry that happened. You had a right to be scared." Bobby turned to leave then twisted back. "Hostellers wouldn't bother you if you were in your car, would they?"

"Not if they didn't want to get run over," said Hal dryly.

"I wanted to ask if you would take my mother to the doctor. You would be safer driving your car," Bobby stated.

"Wait until I call Dr. Burns for an appointment." Hal hunted in her nurse bag for the cell phone and walked over to the clinic door as she poked the buttons, calling for Emma to come from the kitchen to help her. When the receptionist answered, Hal made the appointment and snapped the flap shut. "We can be there at three p.m this afternoon."

Bobby said, "Gute, that is fine."

"As far as I know, the Hostellers don't know about my car. It will help when I drive by the farm if they don't recognize me."

"Just the same Adam and I will ride along with you and my mother as John has asked us to do." Bobby told her as he went out the door.

When Hal turned around, Emma was looking questioningly from Hal to Annie. "Emma, this is Annie Hosteller. She needs our help." Hal gathered supplies out of the cupboard. "Open up a package of butterfly strips. As soon as I clean this cheek wound, you can put the strips on." Hal patted around the wound with saline solution on a swab and tried to smooth out the curled up flesh. "Now the wound's ready for the butterfly strips. I'll go get a pan of warm water. Annie needs to wash up."

When Hal came back, she stopped at the door with the water to watch. As she applied the strips, Emma talked soothingly to the girl in the same tone of voice she used when she talked to the babies. Annie's alert eyes darted one way then the other. She had large, dark brown eyes which, at her age, should have held a look of innocence. Not wild, frightened looks, fearing Emma's every move.

Hal set the water pan down. "Gute job, Emma. Now could you loan Annie one of your nightgowns? She needs to get in bed and rest. Annie, undress and wash up while we wait for Emma to come back."

Hal observed while the girl moved painfully slow to come out of her threadbare dress. She had plenty of bruises all over her body, dark enough to signal she could have internal damage. To add to her troubles, the girl was having her period unless the bleeding was another result of the beating. She'd bled through the back of her dress and down her legs.

Emma came back with the nightgown. While Annie put it on, Hal nodded for Emma to follow her into the living room. "You can take in a pan of cool water and a cloth. Get Annie covered up and tell her she can lay the cloth on her eyes to take down the swelling. I'm going to call the hospital ER, and take that girl in to be checked out. She could be bleeding inside from the beating. Oh, and she needs the sack of sanitary pads in my dresser drawer. Bring her one and put the rest on the table in the spare room so she has them. Scoot the commode out of the corner over by the bed so she doesn't have to walk far and pull the bed down for her. If you have time could you wash her clothes. They are filthy. If you don't get to it right away, it might not matter. Annie isn't going to feel like getting out of bed for a while."

"Should you get involved in this, Hallie? Daed told you the Hostellers were bad," Emma warned.

"I haven't a choice. As a nurse, I have to help her. Besides, they will never think of looking this far away from their farm. They are fully aware Annie isn't able to make it far on foot the shape she's in. I'll bring the car up by the door for her. Get a blanket to put around her while I make a call to the hospital. Don't say anything to her until I'm ready to go. I need to change clothes."

When Hal came back, she said firmly, "Annie, Emma and I are going to help you get in my car. I'm taking you to the doctor to make sure you're all right."

"I'm not going back outside," Annie said stubbornly.

Hal shook her head vigorously. "Jah, you are. You had a bad beating. You need to be checked over. You will be safe enough in my car. Emma, come help me get Annie up."

Annie didn't say another word as Emma and Hal held her up. Once in the car, Hal handed Annie the pillow and blanket she'd stuffed under her arm. "Lie down in the back seat and cover up. You won't be seen that way."

At the hospital, Hal pulled up to the sidewalk as close as she could get to the ambulance entrance canopy. She obeyed the warning sign that said ambulances only and stopped there. She glanced over the seat. "You stay put until I get some help."

The steel emergency doors whooshed as she neared them. At the desk, the day nurse, Mary Jones, glanced up. "Hi, Hal. In a hurry as usual I see."

"As usual, Mary. Need some help getting a patient out of my car. Bring a wheelchair," Hal instructed.

The efficient nurse took off and was back pushing a chair. "What we got?"

"A beating victim. Girl. Maybe sixteen."

They helped Annie into the wheelchair. Mary headed inside with Hal pushing the wheelchair right behind her. "Hal, put her in the first exam room. I'll page the doctor. Wilbur Price is on duty today."

About fifteen minutes later, a short, balding man in his mid fifties, rushed in. "How's it going today, Nurse Hal?"

"Fine for me, but not so good for my patient, Annie Hosteller." Hal nodded at the girl.

The doctor surveyed Annie from head to toe. "I can see that."

"Aside from all the injuries I can see I thought maybe there might be some internal damage," surmised Hal.

"We'll take her down to x-ray and check. Why don't you call Mary in to help me get Annie ready. Go get a cup of coffee. When we're back and done, Mary will come for you," Dr. Price said.

Annie held her hand out in a panic. "Don't leave me."

Hal squeezed her hand to reassure her. "You will be safe with the doctor. Remember no one knows we're here, and Dr. Price won't tell. Will you, Doctor?"

61

"No, I won't tell. No one will harm you while I'm around, young lady," the doctor assured her.

To Hal it seemed like a long time before Mary came back for her. She'd had enough time to drink a second cup of coffee. Finally, Mary popped in. "The doctor examined the girl while he waited for x-ray results. Dr. Price is in the exam room with her now. You can go talk to him."

As Hal started down the hall, the doctor came to meet her. "I want to talk to you away from where the girl can hear us."

Chapter 6

"All right. What did you find?" Hal asked.

The doctor rubbed the back of his neck as he pursed his lips up for a moment. Finally, he said, "Did you know she'd had a baby?"

Hal gasped. "Nah, I thought she was having her period."

"The urine test came back positive. She has a baggy uterus and open cervical. Delivery in the last day or a little more. Other than that, she's taken a bad trouncing from someone. No internal damage. Do you want me to call the sheriff's office to report this?"

Hal thought for a minute. If the doctor reported about Annie's beating to the sheriff that would get back to the Hostellers. They would know Annie was with the Lapp family. So she told what she hoped was a little white lie considering the Hostellers weren't Amish. "No, I'll leave it up to the Amish leaders to decide. You know the Amish doesn't like calling the law in to handle their problems," Hal said.

"I know, but I had to ask. You can take her home any time. Put her to bed and let her rest until she feels like moving again. Right now every movement is sheer torture," Dr. Price said. As Hal moved away, the doctor reached out and stopped her. "Hal, if that girl comes back here in this shape again, I will report this to the sheriff."

"I understand," Hal replied and hurried to get Annie.

It was a little past noon when Hal drove up by the house. Emma was watching from the window. She helped Hal get Annie out of the car.

By the time they reached the living room, Annie was groaning in pain. Hal said, "Annie, we're going to put you in the spare bedroom upstairs. It will seem like a long ways up those stairs, but you need to stay in bed for several days. Sit down in the rocker for a few minutes and rest. You'll need your strength to climb. Emma, come with me." Hal lead the way to the kitchen and peeked at Redbird in her cradle.

Hal stopped Emma by the table. She whispered, "The doctor said Annie had a baby in the last couple days."

"Really!" Emma exclaimed.

"Shhh! Not so loud. I want you to take the cradle up to the spare room with the baby girl in it and leave her by the side of the bed before we take Annie up." Lifting Redbird out of the cradle, Hal said softly, "I'll put Redbird on the couch. She'll be all right there, but John better get me another cradle made before she learns to turn over."

As soon as they entered the bedroom, Annie stopped to stare at the cradle by the bed. The baby flailed her legs and feet, making whimpering sounds.

Hal said, "Oh, I forgot to tell you, you will be sharing the room with this baby. I picked her up along the way yesterday when I made that call at your house. Would you know anything about her?"

"Nah," said Annie sharply.

Hal pointed toward the bed. "As long as you are going to stay with us, while you're in bed you can make yourself useful by watching this baby for us. Emma, make Annie some broth. Drinking will be easier than chewing, and she needs nourishment. Now, Annie, get in bed so I can cover you up. We'll leave you to rest."

In the kitchen, Emma put on the tea kettle to heat. As she

opened a jar of chicken broth, she asked, "Exactly what did the doctor say?"

"She needs rest and time to heal from the beating. No internal injuries which is gute, but getting over giving birth," Hal said.

Emma twisted to look pointedly at Hal. "A coincidence maybe that she has had a baby, and someone left a baby in your buggy while you were at the Hosteller farm?"

"That's what I wondered, too. Fix that broth and tea. I'll take it up to Anne. I want to see if I can get her to talk to me," Hal said

Outside the spare bedroom, Hal shifted the tray close to her body so she could open the door easy encase Annie had dozed off. The girl was sitting on the edge of the bed with her back to the door, humming to the baby softly as she let the infant nurse.

Hal said, "What's her name?"

Annie's back stiffened as she realized she wasn't alone. Without looking around, she answered, "Beth."

Hal went around the bed and placed the tray on the table in the corner. She sat down beside Annie. "Why did you put her in my buggy?"

Annie's voice came out flat. "To keep her from having the same kind of life I had."

"Who is the father?"

Annie's face turned pale behind the bruises. "I can not say."

"Why can't you tell me? I only want to help," Hal implored.

Annie's eyes filled with tears. She said bluntly honest, "It is not that I do not want to tell you. I do not know which man is the father."

Hal felt sick at her stomach. She went over in her mind the things she had seen at the Hosteller farm. Enough that she knew what Annie said was true. The next revolting thought hit her like a ton of bricks. Almost every man on that farm must be related to Annie. She'd heard enough for now. This was not the time to make Annie relive the horrors. She needs to recuperate.

Hal laid her arm gently around Annie's shoulders and felt her flinch. It would take a long time for the girl to be able to trust that the Lapps meant her no harm. "Well, we're glad to know who Beth's mother is. Emma can bring a stack of diapers in, and you take care of her. Put her in bed with you. She will settle down, sleeping next to her mother.

This afternoon, I have to go to the Keim farm and pick up Lovina Keim to take her to the doctor. If you need anything call for Emma. You drink that broth and tea as soon as you're done feeding Beth. You need the nourishment to produce milk for this hungry baby," Hal said patting the baby's blanket.

On the way over to the Keim farm, Hal thought about the conditions of the rest of the women and children at the Hosteller compound. The more she thought about it the angrier she became. Something should be done to stop those men.

When she drove by the Hosteller place, the boy in his late teens, Marvin, was at the mailbox. He waited to cross the road until her car went by. He stretched his neck out like a goose looking for one of those stinky Chinese beetles that had invaded the area when he recognized her. Marvin watched her as far down the road as he could see before she drove over the hill.

When Bobby came out of the house, Hal said excitedly, "Marvin Hosteller was at the mailbox when I went by. I could tell he knew who I was. Just our luck, my being in the neighborhood is no secret now. Let's get your mother in the car and go."

They helped Lovina onto the back seat then Adam and Bobby scooted in on either side of her. As they neared the Hosteller farm, Bobby pointed out an enclosed buggy was coming down the driveway rather fast. "The driver of that buggy means business. You better speed up, Nurse Hal before that buggy gets on the road."

The driver, Henry Hosteller, was looking right at the car. There wasn't any doubt in Hal's mind that he had been watching for her and saw her coming. He flailed the reins across the horse's back, urging him to run faster. The buggy hurled and bounced along the ruts. The horse's ears were back and his mane flying.

Behind the careening buggy, several more men followed on foot, running to keep up.

Bobby cried, "Henry is going to block the road to stop us or try to run you off the road."

"Not if I can help it." Hal gripped the steering wheel and tromped down hard on the accelerator. As the car roared ahead, she heard Lovina mumbling a prayer behind her.

"Faster, Nurse Hal," Bobby shouted. "We have to get past the driveway. Henry is just about to the road."

In a few seconds, the horse was almost to the middle of the road. By that time, Hal was even with the driveway. She laid down on the horn. The loud blaring scared the horse. The horse reared. His flying hooves missed the car by inches as the copper sedan flashed by.

Bobby wiped his sweaty brow with his coat sleeve. "That was close."

Hal looked in the rear view mirror. The frightened horse bolted on across the road and turned the buggy over in the ditch. Men swarmed down into the ditch to rescue the driver. Bobby was twisted in the seat, watching them. Lovina closed her eyes and leaned her head against the back seat, trying to regain her calm demeanor. This time, she prayed a thankful prayer. Adam was smiling encouragingly at Hal as if to say gute job. Hal gave him a weak smile. She wished if Adam approved of her for some reason it could have been for something besides her driving like a maniac.

While Lovina was in the doctor's exam room, Hal sat with her sons in a quiet corner of the waiting room.

"How was Annie when you left home?" Bobby asked.

"She's resting now. I took her to the hospital this morning for x-rays. Didn't want to miss internal injury as badly as she was beaten," Hal explained.

"Was she hurt inside?" Bobby asked worriedly.

"Nah, just bruised and sore on the outside. I took her home

and put her to bed. Dr. Price said let Annie rest until she can move about on her own without pain," Hal told him. "Bobby, did you know Annie just had a baby?"

Bobby looked stunned. "Nah!"

"She hid the baby in my buggy last night when I stopped at the Hostellers. I found the infant when I got home," Hal said.

"What will happen to them?" Bobby wanted to know.

"We will take care of them. I don't think Annie's family will think to look for her with us. She looks like she is going to be a gute mother if she's given the chance," Hal said.

"Gute," Bobby said approvingly.

Hal nodded. "John will have to make us another cradle. Ours is going to be too crowded soon with two growing babies."

Adam took a note pad and pencil from his shirt pocket. He wrote on the pad and handed it to Bobby.

Bobby nodded. "Nurse Hal, Adam wants to know if he can make the cradle to show his gratefulness for you helping Annie."

"You are so thoughtful, Adam. That would so nice of you to do that. I've seen some of your work so I know the cradle will be extra special. Denki," Hal said.

Adam smiled then nudged his brother in the ribs with an elbow and nodded to the opened door.

The nurse called, "Bobby and Adam Keim."

She escorted them to the exam room. Doctor Burns, a kindly older gentleman that always reminded Hal of a grandfather, said Lovina Keim was anemic due to going through menopause. He prescribed iron pills and told her to get out of her sick bed into sunlight. Get up and walk around more, build up an appetite and drink as much liquid as she could. Her stomach pain was nothing more than acid indigestion from not eating enough.

Hal's next worry was the Hosteller men. She still had to drive back by that farm twice. She felt like she should find a way to protect herself and others from them. While she was in town, she had an idea. She told the Keims she had to make a stop before they left town. Hal came out of the store carrying a carton of pepper spray cans.

She put the box down on the floor in front of the passenger seat and took out a can which she handed to Lovina, explaining to her a few squirts from that can would send any Hosteller man running. Lovina started to protest then thought better of it and took the can. She slipped it into her apron pocket.

The Hosteller's broken buggy was still in the ditch on its side harnessed to the dead horse, but there wasn't any sign of people. They all breathed easier when they made it to the Keim house.

Bobby wanted to ride back home with Hal and let Adam pick him up, but Hal refused. "I'm safe enough in my car. I don't think those men will try to stop me again, do you? If they do I'll try to run them over again."

"They would be crazy to try running you off the road again after they saw how brave you were," Bobby said approvingly.

Once she was home, Hal didn't say much while she helped Emma fix supper. She had this feeling it was better to keep quiet than to get into the subject of the Hostellers. She carried a tray up to Annie, picked at the baby a few minutes and let Redbird nurse, waiting for the milking to be done. After supper, Hal went through the motions of assisting Emma with kitchen cleaned up.

When that was done, Emma said, "I can not stand to see Annie wear that old dress again when she feels better. She needs new clothes. I have some material laid back I was going to use for me a dress and apron. Do you think Annie knows how to sew?"

Hal paused. "I imagine she knows how to do almost anything you do, but she isn't in any shape to sew. She is doing good to take care of her baby until she feels better. Even then we might have to move the sewing machine up to her, and it's heavy. Annie doesn't seem to be interested in leaving that room."

"I can make her a dress and apron tonight." Emma took her

material into the kitchen and laid it on the table to cut out the the pieces. When she had that done, she lit a lamp and moved it over to a table by the treadle sewing machine.

The boys were playing a game of battleship. Redbird was fast asleep, and John was reading his bible.

Hal was suddenly weary. This day had been scary enough to wear her out. She wasn't sure how to go about explaining it to John. He wasn't going to be pleased to hear her story. Sooner or later, she knew she'd have to tell him before someone else did. "I'm sure Annie will appreciate you doing that for her, Emma. If I can help let me know. This has been a long day. I think I'll sit down for a while."

As she walked past John, he looked up. His eyes narrowed as Hal eased onto the couch. She sat with her head down and hands in her lap.

"I'd like to hear about that long day you had. Something is wrong." John said intuitively.

"Just no way to pull the wool over your eyes is there. Something is wrong, but you're not going to like it." The treadle sewing machine stopped clacking, and the boys grew silent. Hal told John about her day anyway since the whole family needed to be on guard. She finished by saying, "Those Hosteller men are mean. Just plain mean."

"You should not be on that road anymore. They will be watching for you and angry that you did not stop," John said.

Emma went back to sewing, but she said, "Daed is right. You should not go down that road again."

John puzzled, "I can not think why they would want to do you that way."

"I think they meant to stop me from talking by running me off the road. Joseph Hosteller thinks I know too much. I didn't hide the fact that I was suspicious about his wife's injuries. He may fear I will report him to the sheriff for beating her. He let Henry try to harm me with the Keim family riding with me in my car. How horrible is that?"

"You have no choice but to be careful until we resolve this

matter. We do not want to lose you," John said with meaning.

"John, I know that, but I can't stop nursing visits because of a bunch of evil men. When someone needs my help I'll take the car instead of the buggy. Eli Mast's wife, Mary, asked me at church if I'd come check her out. I need to go see her in the morning. She's going to have a baby. You know them?"

John thought for a moment. "That would be Butcher Ben's Eli and his Mary. All right, but you make sure one of us knows where you are at all times when you leave home. You will be traveling away from the Hosteller farm to the Mast farm, but that is little solace right now," John declared.

"I'll make sure one of you knows where I've gone. I don't want to tangle with the men from that compound again. Today Annie told me the most horrid thing. She has no idea which one of those men is her baby's father. Is this what you called being different, John? I call it evil. We need to do something about that compound. It's a horrible prison for the women and children who live there. Think what it's doing to the mind of the children growing up in that environment."

"Do the children get any schooling?" Emma wondered as she fed material under the sewing machine foot feed.

"I didn't see a building that looked like a school. From the look of the adults, I don't think any of them are educated. Annie may not be able to write and read," Hal said.

"While she is living with us, I will give her some lessons," Emma said.

"Daniel and me will be glad to help," Noah added.

"I think that is a gute idea. Annie needs all the help she can get. John, Dr. Price wanted to call the sheriff department and fill out a complaint for Annie, but I told him to wait. I wasn't sure what you would want to do."

John frowned. "Going to the law to press charges against a person is not our way. We should fight cruelty with kindness and forgiveness."

"I knew that, but you said yourself these people aren't part of the Plain community," Hal said. "I didn't know if that made a difference."

"It does not matter if it is a Plain person or Englischers," John said.

"The cruelty on that farm must be stopped somehow. If the Hostellers find Annie and the baby here, they will make her go back home with them. She is underage so Joseph has a right to take her from this house. I can't bare to think about her and the baby in that awful place, and those men repeating the same offenses. We need to think of something to help all of them," Hal pleaded. "Actually, it's my duty as a health care worker to report matters like this as child abuse. Doctor Price said if Annie were to come back to the ER in the condition she was this morning he'd report it to the law."

"I do not know what we should do, but I am inclined to agree with you. I will talk to Bishop Elton tomorrow. It would be best if he made the decision," John said.

"I'm serious about the place being a prison. I saw a man locked in a chicken house when I was there. If Nonnie Hosteller is any example, that poor woman is scared to death. The other women and children must be treated the same way and need help to get away from there. Only the law can handle this problem," Hal declared.

"We will sleep on this tonight and worry fresh in the morning," John said. "You look like you need a good night's sleep."

"That I do," Hal agreed.

In the middle of the night, a piercing shriek caused John and Hal to sit up in bed. They gave each other a wide eyed look.

"What was that?" John asked.

Hal patted her chest. "Phew! I don't know."

Chapter 7

A mournful wail echoed down the hall followed by hard sobbing. "That must be Annie." The outburst woke up baby Beth. Startled, she cried right along with her mother.

Hal slipped out of bed. "I'll go see to her, John. Go on back to sleep."

As Hal past the boys room, Noah said sleepily, "Is everything all right, Mama Hal?"

"I think Annie had a bad dream. Go back to sleep."

By the time she got to Annie's door, Emma was out in the hall, coming to meet her. "That sure scared me," she whispered.

"All of us," Hal said as she opened the bedroom door. "Annie, it's Hal and Emma."

The girl quieted down when she heard Hal speak. Emma went around the bed, lit the lamp and picked up the baby from beside Annie. "There, there, little one," she cooed. She snuggled the baby next to her shoulder and patted her on the back.

Hal sat down beside Annie. The girl sniffed. "I – I'm sorry I disturbed all of you." She shivered and pulled the cover up around herself.

"Are you cold? Would you like another quilt?" Hal asked.

Annie swallowed hard. "I feel like I'm freezing and sick to my stomach every time I wake up from a nightmare."

"Ah. Do you have bad dreams often?" Hal took the hanky laying beside Annie's pillow and dabbed at the tears rolling down the girl's cheeks.

Annie nodded yes. Her voice quivered with emotion. "I thought maybe now that I am somewhere I know I am safe the nightmares would stop. Fear just never leaves me."

"That will take time. Right now the memories are too fresh," Hal said, patting Annie's hand. "Think you can go back to sleep now?"

"I'll try," Annie murmured.

Emma laid the sleeping baby back on the bed and took a quilt out of the storage closet. She spread the cover over Annie. "Would you like me to sleep with you? I am pretty gute at keeping away bad dreams."

Annie, without hesitation, said, "I would like that."

Before daylight, John's alarm clock buzzed at 5 a.m. He slept right through it and so did Hal. The break of day entering the windows put everyone on their feet at the same time and on the run to get caught up with chores and get breakfast out of the way.

Right after breakfast, John came from the barn to greet Elton Bontrager as he stopped his buggy in front of the house.

Hal greeted Elton at the door.

John said, "I was going to come see you this morning. Come sit at the table. We need to talk."

Elton asked as he followed John to the kitchen, "Why did you want to see me?"

"About the Hostellers."

As Hal poured them a cup of coffee, Elton said, "They are the reason why I came here. The Hosteller men attacked one of their neighbors in the middle of the night last night, Hamish and Edna Manwiller. They yanked the couple out of bed and held them down while they cut Hamish's beard off with battery operated scissors. When they finished with him, they cut

Edna's hair off as short as they could. The Manwillers came to see me this morning. Understandably, they are very upset and humiliated by this. Like the rest of us Hamish believes in be not overcome with evil but overcome evil with gute, but this shaming cruelty was almost more than they could bear."

Hal sank into a chair across the table. "Those men knew what it means for Plain men to grow a beard and women to never cut their hair. Why would they do such a degrading thing to two nice people?"

Elton explained, "Hamish says Joseph has been to see him several times. Since Hosteller's land joins the Manwiller farm, Joseph tried to talk the Manwillers into joining his group and putting his land in with theirs. Hamish keeps turning him down, and Joseph leaves angry every time. Although, joining the Hosteller community did not come up last night."

"Joseph Hosteller is one scary man, and not one to be cross easily," Hal surmised.

"That seems to be true. Joseph was not with his sons and grandsons when they invaded the Manwiller house. He sent them to do his dirty work for him. They were looking for Joseph's daughter. She ran away from home. Hamish said Henry and Eli were sure the girl was hidden in their house. When Hamish denied it, the men beat him and disfigured him and his wife. After they were tortured, Hamish and Edna still denied hiding the girl. The men would not believe them until after they searched the house."

John looked at Hal questioningly.

"Tell him," she said.

"Elton, the girl is with us." John went on to explain the circumstances.

Elton said, "Your family will be in danger if Joseph Hosteller finds out. We must not let word of this get out. I suspect they will not give up. No telling who they will attack next, searching for the girl. They know the Amish community does not agree with their ways so they have no regard for any of us.

We all have to be careful. I will spread the word no Sunday evening teenage singings and no church meetings. It is just as well that it is time for school to be out. We do not want the Hostellers to stop lone buggies on the road. Hal, you can not go out alone until this matter is settled."

"I won't take the buggy out alone," she agreed. "I've had all the confrontations with Joseph Hosteller that I want. But if you have no objections when I make a nursing visit, I'd like to use my car. I need to pay a visit to Mary Mast this morning."

"That is fine. We need you safe," Elton said.

"But what about Easter?" John asked.

"That's right. Everyone looks forward to the Easter service," Hal agreed.

"I dislike that this family can disrupt our preaching service at Easter when we want to celebrate Christ is Risen. I do not think the Hostellers would bother us in a large group, but getting back and forth to church, we are strung out and outnumbered if the Hostellers strike."

John said, "What if we went to church in groups? If we stick together in numbers we should be safer."

Elton hesitated for a moment to think. "That should work. Before other incident happens, I am going to have a talk with Joseph Hosteller this morning. I doubt he will listen to reason, but as bishop it is my job to try."

"Elton, you can not go to that compound alone. I will go with you," John declared.

"I do appreciate the offer. Can you go now?"

"Jah, I can."

On the ride to the Hosteller farm, John told Elton how the Hostellers used a buggy to try to run Hal off the road when she was taking the Keim family to the doctor and Henry, drunk in the salebarn, was made to leave. "The men forced Hal go to Joseph's house. His wife had been beaten. She claimed she fell, but Hal thought different."

"We have closed our eyes to all the despicable, horrifying things that has been going on. When the violence happens to our people, because Joseph Hosteller is so bold with his deeds thinking we will remain quiet, it is time to stop him if we can. First, we will try talking to him," Elton said.

When they pulled into the long driveway men were out in the fields. Women hoed and planted in the large communal garden. Children worked along side their parents. Their attire would lead any Englischer to believe that they were Amish. The men wore beards, but none of the women had on a prayer cap.

Those that heard the buggy coming by them stopped what they were doing and stared with hollow, vacant eyes until the buggy past by. Mangy, emaciated dogs burst from behind buildings and rushed the buggy, yipping at the wheels on both sides.

"Elton, I do not see one building that looks like a school for all the children here," John said. "Hal thinks the children can not read or write."

"Just one more aggression against Joseph and his sons. If he keeps his people from education, they are more dependent on the Hostellers."

Elton halted in front of Joseph's house. The men stepped down and looked around, wondering where they might find the elderly leader. The dogs circled them, barking and sniffing.

From behind the buggy came Henry Hosteller and his son, Marvin. Henry, a cigarette dangling from his mouth, stopped in front of the bishop and said menacingly, "Look, son, we have company. What do you think is the reason after all this time the bishop would come to visit?"

Marvin uttered a mirthless laugh. "Can not say."

Henry twisted around and yelled, "Shut up, you blasted dogs. We can not hear for you." The dogs, no doubt, knew what tormenting punishment would befall them if they didn't obey. They slinked away at a trot with their tails between their legs.

Glaring down at Elton, Henry got to the point, "What do you want here, Bishop?"

Elton held his ground. "I have come to talk to Joseph

Hosteller."

"Marvin, take these men to the house," Henry ordered and walked away.

Marvin walked briskly to the house with the men following him. The boy knocked on the door and heard a rough, "Come in." He opened the door. "Bishop Bontrager and another man is here to see you."

"Let them in," Joseph snapped.

Elton and John blinked their eyes a few times to get used to the dim room. Joseph was seated in a rocker. He didn't offer to get up or shake hands with them. He pointed at the threadbare couch. "Sit down if you like."

"Denki, but we are not going to stay very long," Elton said. "I am here as bishop for this area. This is John Lapp. We want to talk to you."

The only sign that he recognized the name Lapp was when Hosteller's eyebrows went up. "Talk!" It was not a polite request but a gruff order.

Elton cleared his throat and entwined his fingers. Not one thing was easy about confronting this man. "It has been reported to me that your sons and grandsons invaded the Manwiller house. They did harm to the couple. Do you deny that?"

"I can not say what happened when my sons visited the Manwillers. I was not with them and have not discussed the visit with them. My youngest daughter has disappeared. I told her brothers to go around to the neighboring farms to look for her. That is all I know," Joseph said with a shrug.

John said bluntly, "Explain to us why Henry tried to run my wife off the road when she past your driveway?"

"I did hear something about that," Joseph said, smirking. "Henry said the horse ran away with him. Unfortunately, he had not gotten it under control when Nurse Hal happened by. We lost a good buggy and horse. What Henry told me was Nurse Hal tried to run into his horse with her car."

Rage was building in John. He had to fight to keep from

78

looking angry. "We do not believe that is so."

Joseph pounded the arm of his rocker with his fist. "I believe my son!"

Elton said quietly, "There is one other thing we want you to believe. Our community will not stand for the same treatment that you serve out to your members here. We do not intend to sit by and let you treat our people in the shameful manner you did the Manwillers."

Joseph's angry eyes tried to bore a hole through Elton. "My concern is my lost daughter. If she were to return home, there would be no need to bother our neighbors. Tell me, Bishop, have you seen my daughter, Annie?"

John looked at the wall as he waited to see how Elton answered. Elton believed John's family would be in danger for harboring Annie, but it was not in his nature to lie. It was not the Plain way.

Elton said firmly, "Nah, I have not seen your daughter. Why did she run away?"

"I do not know," was Joseph's reply.

Elton returned with meaning, "If I do see her I will be sure to ask her."

Joseph put his hands down on the arms of his chair and pushed himself up. He eyed them warily. "This visit is over." Then he ended the visit by walking out of the room.

As they drove down the driveway, Eli Hosteller rushed from row to row in the garden, yelling at the women huddled together. He shook his iron fist at their faces. "There's no time to rest. Get a move on. You can work faster than this. We have much more to get done before dark." The women separated and with bowed heads went back to work.

John said sadly, "I see those women in Annie. Now I understand why Annie is that way."

"Jah, the men keep their followers scared to death. Makes them easier to control," Elton surmised.

"Annie and her baby are wilkcum to live with us as members of our family. Elton, the girl could use counciling from you.

She knows no other way of live except to be mistreated and shamed. What they have done to her tortures her even when she is asleep."

"Annie is just one of many in that community that need help," Elton said flatly.

"Can we help these poor people, Bishop? There must be a way to save them from the Hostellers," John said perplexed.

"That just might be the result of what happens by saving our community from those men. Though I fear it will be at the cost of our belief to treat grievances against us with forgiveness. I will make that decision when the time comes. I tell you this, I will not stand by and let the Hostellers terrorize this community. We should not have to be prisoners in our own homes and live in fear of them."

"I agree, Elton. I got to admit I was getting ready to run for the door when Joseph Hosteller asked if you knew where his daughter was. I thought for sure you would feel you had to tell the truth."

Elton chuckled. "I forgive you for your lack of faith in my convictions, my friend. But if you had been paying attention I did not lie. Joseph asked me if I had seen Annie. Not did I know where she was. I told the truth. I have not seen her yet."

"That is right. Did you see the sore mark you hit with the man when you asked why Annie ran away? He fears Annie will tell all the degrading evils that he and his sons heap on those poor followers and his own family," John said.

"Jah, and that is why they think they have no choice but to terrorize the community until they find Annie or someone tells them where to look. John, we have to warn everyone to lock their doors and be prepared. These men will strike again," Elton predicted.

"I can go with you to do that. The Hostellers will not be afraid of Plain people. They think they know our peaceful ways will not let us fight back. We need to do more for protection. I am for telling the men to keep their hunting rifles and shotguns handy and sleep lightly."

"As much as I hate this, I approve. John, most Plain houses do not have locks on the doors. We must tell people to buy locks right away," Elton planned.

"That may not stop strong, rough men but at least the noise of breaking in will wake up the households if this happens again. Even then I fear the Hostellers will not be stopped," John said.

Elton shook his head in agreement. "I felt so sorry for the Manwillers. I asked Hamish if he wanted to press charges and he said no. He said if we practice what we preach we must remain pacifists no matter what. He did add he would rather have had the beating twice as rough rather than the shameful disfigurement done to him and his wife."

Chapter 8

After John and Elton left the house, Emma said she wanted to take a walk through the timber, looking for wild herbs to make cold and flu medicines out of. Hal tried to convince her that antibodies would work better and faster, but Emma was insistent she needed to pick herbs to have on hand.

As soon as Emma took off with her basket, Hal went upstairs to sit with Annie a few minutes. "Bishop Bontrager has just left."

"Does he know me and the baby are here?" Annie asked frantically.

"We told him, but he won't tell anyone. He understands that you are in danger. He came to tell us your older brothers and their sons beat up the Manwillers in the night, searching for you. They thought Hamish was hiding you. When he said you weren't there, they cut off his beard and Edna's hair."

"Oh, those poor people. I know they were really scared," Annie said woefully.

"Scared and humiliated by being disfigured like that. I don't know how much you understand about Amish belief. Plain men believe once they marry they should always have a beard like Jesus. Hamish feels he has been disfigured. Women can never cut their hair and must always wear a prayer cap to cover their heads. Edna Manwiller feels she has been shamed in everyone's eyes, because her hair was cut. Annie, the men in your family have to be stopped. Would you consider going to the sheriff to press charges?"

Annie was horrified by the thought. "I can not do that. Papa would know where I am living and come get me. It is not safe for Beth and me in his house now that he is angry. You saw what he did to Mama when he was drinking. It is much worse when he is revengeful. He will not tolerate someone disobeying him"

"You and your mother aren't the only ones hurt. I saw a man locked in a chicken house when I was leaving that night. He shouldn't be made to live in there."

"That is the way Papa punishes the other men when they disobey him. He usually makes the men stay in there ten or twelve days. Sometimes, I think Papa makes more out of the punishment he gives the men for a reason. While they are confined, Papa sleeps with their wives and excuses his actions by saying he is cleansing them of the devil.

Some of the men are my father's cousins, and some are not related. Not all of them believe Papa is right, but they are forced to obey him, because they can not get away from him," Anna said. "The women obey Papa and my brothers, because they are afraid not to."

"Like your mother?"

"Jah, like her and me. My father is an evil man," Annie told her as she hugged Beth close to her.

"Joseph sees to it his followers fear him. Is what happened to the Manwillers the sort of thing that made your father move everyone here from Pennsylvania?"

"Jah, we have moved several times when he and the others got in trouble with the law. I always hoped that the law would stop them from hurting us, but that has never happened," Annie said resignedly.

"Maybe this will turn out all right once Elton and John warn everyone to be on guard against your father. Maybe he will move his community somewhere else when he sees the Plain people in this community are going to stand up to him. Only that doesn't help the poor people who don't want to be apart of his group anymore," surmised Hal. "Now I have to go on a home visit this morning. Emma is in the timber, looking for medicinal herbs. You will be in the house alone for awhile. Will that be all right?"

"Jah, I will be fine. Beth and me are safe in this room. You go do what you have to do," Annie assured her.

Where she was headed to Eli Mast's farm was in the opposite direction from the Hosteller farm. At the intersection, Hal turned north and tried to console herself with the idea that nothing would happen to her. Most of those awful men were in jail. Any others not arrested should be afraid to retaliate for fear of winding up in jail themselves. The sheriff said so. Still in all, she knew she and all the others in the Plain community were getting a taste of the fear that Annie had lived with all those years.

John had given Hal good directions to an area of flat, rich, river bottom land. She slowed down to read the mailbox and found she had the right place. She drove past long rows of corn and stopped by the house. Like all the other Amish farmsteads in the area, this one was kept up and neat.

Fair haired, blue eyed Mary Mast waited on the porch for her, waving and wearing a big smile. Her thin frame was sway backed now, off balanced by the baby bump. She appeared to be only a couple of years older than Emma. "Gute morning, Nurse Hal," she called, resting her arms across her chest as most Amish women did when they relaxed.

"Gute morning, Mary. Nice day, ain't?"

"Jah, come in. I just finished cleaning a bunch of vegetables for a kettle of soup and put it on the stove. Trying to get rid of last summer's vegetables now that it is time to plant garden again. We will go to the kitchen so I can stir my soup while we talk," the young woman said, leading the way. "You are wilkcum to stay for dinner if you have the time."

"Denki, from the gute smell coming out of that soup kettle, I think this is the best offer I've had for awhile," Hal replied. "Before you get any busier, I should give you that check up. It won't take long. I'll need you to lie down on the bed for me."

Mary nodded. "Follow me."

Hal walked behind Mary through her spotless house to the bedroom. "How have you been feeling?" If Mary's industriousness was any indication, she must be feeling well.

Hal did her examination and helped Mary sit up on the edge of the bed. "I make it that you are five months along."

"Jah, that is how I make it," Mary said cheerfully. "I am so glad we found a place of our own and moved from my folks home before the baby comes. It is so good that Eli and me have our own home to start our family in."

"Is there anything that you want to ask me?" Hal asked.

As with most girls Mary hadn't had any sex education. What experience she had about birthing babies or taking care of one had to be from helping her mother with younger siblings. Most of the time, young brides in a first time pregnancy were clueless about what was happening to their bodies and what to expect when labor hit them. Mothers wouldn't share that kind of information. When she asked one Amish mother why daughters weren't better prepared, she had been told it was not done. That was their way, and that was the only explanation given.

Mary thought for a second. "Nah, no questions. I have to stir my soup now." She pushed herself up off the bed and went to a small table nearby. "First, let me show you what I made for the baby so far." She picked up folded white baby garments and handed the stack to Hal. On top was a dainty bonnet.

Hal unfolded the top gown and held it up with the white bonnet. "These are so very sweet, and you have done such a neat job of sewing the clothes. Your baby will be proud to wear them."

Mary beamed with joy as she led Hal back to the kitchen.

Eli, as dark as his wife was fair, came to meet them from the kitchen. His chin sprouted dark stubble that would turned into a beard. "Gute morning, Nurse Hal. How are you?"

"I'm fine. So is your wife. In about four months, you are going to be a father," Hal told him.

The soon to be father grinned from ear to ear. "That is gute."

"Once a month, you bring Mary by the clinic so I can check her unless you need me before that. Is there a phone shed close by?"

"Jah," Eli said. "Just east of us on the corner."

"I'll keep my cell phone charged and handy so you can reach me day or night. Mary, I'll take that drink now. Hope you don't mind Eli. Your wife invited me to dinner."

"If I did it is too late now," he said dryly. Puzzled by that response, Hal stopped and gave Eli a studied look. He chuckled at her reaction. "You are always wilkcum here."

That was the first time, Hal was caught off guard by Eli's sense of humor, but after that, she was prepared for him. In fact, it was a good feeling to know this young Amish man would tease her. She felt like she had been accepted.

At dawn the next morning, the Lapp family woke to pounding on the front door. Hal and Emma followed John down the stairs. He picked up his hunting rifle and cracked the door open. "Bobby Keim, come in," he said in alarm.

Hal and Emma rushed to the young man when he staggered and collapsed against the wall.

"Emma, get a chair," John said as he helped Hal hold Bobby up.

Annie came out of hiding in the upstairs hall and followed the boys downstairs. She rushed to Bobby and took his hand. She asked angrily, "You are hurt. Did my brothers do this to you?"

Bobby shook his head yes.

"Your mother and Adam, are they all right?" Hal asked in concern.

"They were not harmed."

"Gute," Hal said. "Did you mother get a chance to use the

pepper spray on them?"

Bobby tried to grin and grimaced instead. "Nah. The men didn't bother Mama. They know she is not well, and Adam can not talk so he was of no use to them. But they meant for me to tell them if I had Annie hidden out." He took Annie's hand. "I told them she was not in our house, but they beat me anyway before they searched the house."

"I am so sorry they hurt you, Bobby. This is all my fault," Annie said, kneeling beside him.

Hal noted the look of worried concern that passed between them. She'd have to find a time to ask Annie just how well she knew Bobby Keim.

Bobby shook his head at Annie. "This is not your fault. Those men do not have the right to beat me."

John said, "Bobby, they have got to be stopped. Will you go tell the sheriff what has happened?"

"We can not accuse them and get them arrested, can we? That is not our way," Bobby said in frustration.

"Even if you do not press charges, the sheriff needs to know what is going on out here. Maybe he can help us before anyone else is beaten and disfigured. Go warn the Hostellers to leave us alone. Bishop Bontrager said our going to the law would be what we needed to do if the Hostellers invaded another home," John insisted.

Hal added, "Bobby, it is a gute idea. Standing up to them will keep them from harming someone else. The Hosteller men attacked your neighbors, the Manwillers, looking for Annie. They will continue from farm to farm looking for her and hurting Plain people."

Bobby asked, "Will you go with me to the sheriff's office, John Lapp?"

John started for the door. "Jah. Let's go now and pick up Bishop Bontrager. He will want to go with us."

While John and Bobby were gone most of the morning, Noah and Daniel did chores. Emma and Hal hoed in the garden for awhile. Hal said she was hungry for rhubarb pie. Emma

87

declared her back was aching from bending over so long. She decided it was time they straightened up and walked around the house to the back fence to see how tall the rhubarb plants were. Both of them were disappointed when Emma said she thought the stalks needed to be a little longer.

When Bobby dropped John off, Emma asked him and Elton to stay for dinner, but they refused. Bobby said his mother and Adam would worry about him until he returned home safe. Elton agreed that Jane would be uneasy, too.

John sat down at the table and explained to Hal and Emma that the sheriff said attacking Amish people was considered a hate crime. Bobby and the Manwillers would not have to press charges. The sheriff was going to get the FBI involved. Agents would come out to investigate. Once the Manwillers and Bobby told their stories, that was enough for the FBI to raid the Hosteller farm and arrest the men. Just looking at Hamish's hacked beard and his wife's clipped hair, plus the bruises on both Hamish and Bobby would be enough for the FBI to know the men were telling the truth.

That afternoon, Hal made an appointment with Dr. Burns to have a check up for Annie and the baby. She went up to Annie's room to tell her about the doctor appointment. Annie was standing off to the side, peering at the road over the half curtain. She stiffened when she heard Hal enter her room and only relaxed when she saw who it was. She walked so softly in her room they were never able to hear her footsteps. She remained on edge and stood for hours, staring out the window as if always watchful for danger. Annie resembled a half wild kitten that hesitated, studying her surroundings for danger.

"Annie, there's no reason to worry. You're safe. There's nothing to see out that window, is there?"

Annie gave her a small smile. "Right now I am watching Daniel down on his hands and knees in front of a little turkey. A setting hen and chicks are circling around them, looking upset. Daniel looks to be in danger. Can you explain that?"

"Why don't you come sit on the bed by me? Rest and I'll tell you the story," Hal said, patting the quilt. "You remember me saying I bought a box of chicks at the salebarn for Emma to put under a setting hen? We didn't know there was a baby turkey in the box when I bid on it. Not that it matters. The hen didn't know the difference between Tom and her other adopted baby chicks any more than I did when I bought them. Now Daniel has taken a liking to Tom. Since the turkey has outgrown the setting hen, Daniel is making a pet out of him.

Annie, I've been wondering about something. Why did you pick the Keim farm to run to that night in the rain? How did you know that would be a safe place to go?"

Annie concentrated on her hands in her lap. "Sometimes when I could not take being in the house with Mama any longer, I would slip away and go for a walk. Once in awhile, Bobby would be fixing fence or checking his stock cows when I got to our fence line. He was always so nice to talk to. I got to hoping he would be there every time I took a walk, but he was not always."

"I see. Is there any chance that Bobby is your baby's father?" Hal asked bluntly.

Annie shook her head as tears welled in her eyes. "Nah, Bobby is not like them."

"Why pick Bobby Keim to run to?"

"Come right down to it I did not have a choice if I wanted to save myself. As hurt as I was walking much farther would have been hard to do. Bobby and me just talked a few times. I do not think I would even say we were friends. Bobby was kind me, and I felt safe with him. I remembered that when I needed a place to hide."

"What made your brothers think you might be at the Manwiller farm?"

Annie shrugged. "I can not say for sure. Once in awhile, I rode along with Papa when he stopped to talk to Hamish about joining our group. Maybe he thought having his child along would be what might soften the Manwillers up agree with him. Edna Manwiller always gave me cookies and milk while the men talked. She was nice to me. My father would remember a thing like that. The Manwillers live close so I guess that was why Papa sent my brothers there first, thinking that is where I would go."

"Annie, you need to start telling yourself you're safe now," Hal said, putting an arm around the girl's trembling shoulders.

Annie's eyes filled with tears. "Nurse Hal, I am sorry. Fear has been with me so long. I think it will never leave me as long as my father and brothers are free to hunt me down.

You have such a warm family. I want to trust you and be comfortable here for whatever time my baby and me are allowed to stay. If only I could forget, but that will never happen. Even in my sleep I live the horrors."

"I know. Time has a way of helping lessen the fear and living with people you can trust helps." Placing her hand under the girl's chin, Hal turned Annie's face toward her. "About that, John and I discussed your situation. We made a decision, but in this family we take a vote just to make sure all of us are in agreement. I know it's not the usual Plain way, but it works for the Lapp family. We want you to live with us for as long as you want. You and Beth will be a part of this family if you would like to be."

Annie broke into tears. "I would like that very much. I could not imagine what was to become of Beth and me. I have worried so much about that."

"You can stop worrying and dry those tears. We are like the setting hen. John and I have learned of late that we can't tell chicks Annie and Beth from our other chicks. But you should know, as part of this family, sooner or later Emma and I expect you to come out of this room and start helping us take care of this family. Everyone had to do their share, but we are willing to wait until you're ready," Hal said. "Now get prepared for that trip to the doctor."

Annie's voice quivered. "I do not think it is a gute idea to be going anywhere in your car. What if my father or brothers saw us on the road?"

"If you lie down in the back seat like you did before no one will know you're in the car with me. We will be back home before you know it," Hal said.

Before they got in the car, Hal handed Annie a spray can. "Take this and stick it in your pocket."

"What is it?"

"Pepper spray. If you spray anyone in the face with it, their eyes and face will burn and hurt. Changes their mind in a hurry about what they had planned to do," Hal assured her.

With a determined upward tilt of her chin, Annie slipped the spray in her pocket.

When Hal and Annie arrived home, John met them at the door. "Sheriff Dawson and a FBI agent are here. They want to talk to both of you."

Annie had fear plastered all over her face. She whispered hoarsely to Hal, "They are going to make me go home."

"Nah, they can't do that," Hal said. "Just listen to what they have to say." She crossed the room to the couch with John and Annie behind her. The two men stood up, one in a tan uniform with a star on his chest and the other in a dark suit."

John introduced, "This is my wife, Hallie and Annie Hosteller."

The tall man in the uniform had sharp, observing eyes. Hal doubted that he missed much when he looked for a reaction from a suspect. "I'm Jeff Dawson, and this is FBI agent Mack Summers."

The agent had a pleasant, boyish face and curly black hair. He nodded and gave them a friendly smile meant to put them at ease.

Hal said, "Sit down, gentlemen, while we talk. John and I will get us some chairs from the kitchen."

Once they were all seated, Hal said to the sheriff, "What brings you here?"

"We wanted Miss Hosteller to know that Bobby Keim gave us a statement about the Hosteller men attacking him. He told us about the life that Annie has been forced to live at that compound. However, Bobby was reluctant to press charges because of Amish beliefs. Hamish Manwiller told us the same thing. We respect that.

We understand Joseph Hosteller has tried to force his followers on the Amish church with the thought that he might be able to force more Amish members to join his group. From what we've found out about the Hostellers. What they are really after is other farms to put in their names.

Now Joseph has a grudge against the Amish community for not accepting his offer of combining with his family. The assaults that have occurred are considered hate crimes against the Amish community. As such, I called in the FBI to help my department arrest the Hosteller men."

Agent Summers said, "Miss Hosteller, we have arrested your father, brothers and two cousins. They are in jail, charged with Civil Rights violations. A hearing date will be set. If any of the Amish attacked want to testify we'd appreciate the help. Bobby Keim is going to testify about the beating Henry and Eli gave him. Living as close as his family does to the compound, the Keims will feel safer if those men are put in prison for a good long time." Annie slumped over with her head down. The FBI agent continued, "Miss Hosteller, a hearing is to determine if your relatives should be brought to trial for crimes they have been accused of. We are asking anyone they harmed if they will testify at the hearing. We are well aware of the horrible conditions on the Hosteller farm. We could send those men away for even longer if we had an eye witness to tell at the hearing about the deplorable conditions at the farm. You could testify and help free all those poor followers including your mother."

Annie shook her head fast. "Nah, nah. I can not. I am too scared. My father and the others still do not know where I am living. I want to keep it that way. You do not have all of the men arrested that harmed me. I am still in danger as long as they are free."

The FBI agent nodded. "I understand. We don't blame you

for being scared. Would you tell us the names of the other men that we haven't arrested yet?"

"I can not," Annie said tearfully.

Agent Summers said, "This should work out all right in the end. With Mr. Keim and the Manwillers statement and Mr. Keim's testimony we should have enough evidence to get the men brought to trial and sentenced. Maybe in the mean time, someone else will step forward to testify against the Hostellers."

Sheriff Dawson added, "If not, we can hope that with the leaders in prison, the rest of the group won't try to break the law on their own."

The Easter Sunday church meeting was the turn of Butcher Ben Mast and his wife, Edna. The Lapps were up early to get ready. Emma offered to stay home with Annie, but Annie refused to let her. She said Nurse Hal kept telling her she was safe, and she had to try to believe that. The Lapp family should all go to church to celebrate Easter.

Bishop Bontrager quoted from the bible, "These seven things the Lord hates; a proud look, a lying tongue, hands that shed innocent blood, a heart that devises wicked plans, feet that are swift in running to evil, a false witness who speaks lies and one who sows discord among brethren." He looked around the room before he said, "Does this passage not sound like it was directed toward some men we know? Sooner or later, the reign of such men comes to an end as it has for the Hostellers."

The day passed without a problem from the remaining Hosteller men that were still free. However, Plain men saw the wisdom in sticking close together while traveling in a parade of buggies to church and back to home.

Chapter 9

When the word passed through the Easter church meeting that Hostellers men were in jail, Plain people relaxed. Life was almost back to normal by May. Church meetings and Sunday night teenagers buddy group singings were not a cause for worry.

Hearing all that had taken place didn't make a difference as far as Annie's fears went. She refused to come out of her bedroom. She continued to pace the floor, sorrowfully burdened by her memories and the never ending nightmares that woke her in the middle of the night. On those nights, Hal or Emma got out of bed to comfort her until she fell back to sleep.

Hal hadn't been able to persuade Annie to join the family downstairs. The girl was always fearful that some awful calamity would befall her and her baby if she didn't hide in her room.

One morning as soon as they had the dishes washed, Hal slipped her dish towel over the bar and announced to Emma, "I'm going upstairs and tell Annie you're fixing the bath water for the babies. I'm going to tell her she needs to come down to the kitchen and give Beth her bath."

Emma squeezed the dish cloth dry and hung it beside the

towel. "She has let me bathe the baby until now. You think she will listen to you?"

"Something had to be done to snap her out of the state she's in. I told her we'd give her some time, but she's had long enough. Just suggesting she take a part in this family hasn't worked. Maybe we just need to jump start her. We'll begin small and work up. Annie won't come out of that room for herself, but she might for her baby's sake." Hal marched upstairs and into Annie's bedroom. "Annie, we need to give our babies their bath right now."

Annie turned from the window, sensing Hal's urgency. "Go head and take her," she said, nodding toward the new cradle Adam built for Beth.

"I can't do it. I'm bathing Redbird. You need to bath your own baby."

"Emma can bathe the baby. She always does," Annie said.

"Emma has plenty of her own work to do. She can't always do our work, too. She's getting ready to go to the garden to hoe and bring in radishes and lettuce to clean for dinner. Now come along," Hal said and wheeled out of the room.

While Hal laid Redbird on the blanket she'd spread on the table, Emma put water in one of the two pans. "Well?"

Hal looked behind her and whispered, "I don't know. I left before she had time to say no." She undressed Redbird and under her breath said, "I hope she comes. I'm running out of ideas."

Hal eased Redbird into the pan. As she washed, the baby let out with a hoarse laugh, and Hal laughed with her. "Emma, she sounds like that young rooster of yours."

When Emma didn't reply, Hal glanced at her. Emma was staring at the doorway. Behind Hal, Annie said, "This other pan for Beth."

"Jah," Hal said as Emma rushed for water to put in the pan.

Trying to make it seem as if this was the normal routine for both of them, Hal kept washing Redbird and picking at her to make the bath enjoyable. Redbird giggled and cooed in response.

When Annie's baby sunk in the warm water, she whimpered. "Beth does not like to take a bath." Annie complained. "She is not happy like Redbird."

Fearing that would be the excuse Annie needed to dry Beth off and go back to her bedroom, Emma said, "That's strange. When I give Beth her bath she does not mind. Hallie, I'm going to find my hoe now."

Annie frowned at Emma's back as she left. The remark didn't set well.

Realizing the girl needed to learn how to be a mother, Hal advised, "Annie, babies are sensitive to the people they're with. They sense their mother's mood. If you want Beth to think it's fun to take a bath, you have to smile and pick at her to keep her attention off bathing just like I'm doing with Redbird. It's as simple as that."

Annie watched Hal continue to pick at Redbird while she swiped the wet cloth over the baby's head and said, "Peek a boo." That brought giggles from the baby.

Soon Annie was doing the same to her baby. With each quick smile, giggles or laugh from the infant, Annie grew more confident and at ease about giving her baby a bath.

Hal dried Redbird and sat down to hold her while Annie finished Beth's bath. As soon as the baby was wrapped in her blanket, Annie picked her up, ready to leave.

"Lay the baby down on the table by me so you can empty both the bath pans. Just throw the water out the back door and dry the pans out and put them back on the counter. The wash cloths and towels go in the dirty clothes basket in the mud room. The baby shampoo, powder and soap goes in the clinic cupboard."

Annie hesitated. Hal could tell she really wanted to say no and leave. Without a word, the girl laid her baby on the table in front of Hal and did the clean up while Hal picked at Beth and Redbird. Annie sped through the task, picked her baby up and started out the door.

"Annie."

"Jah," the girl said wearily, fearing what other tasks might be coming.

Hal didn't turn around to face her. "Emma and I are far too busy to keep carrying you a tray and cleaning your commode. You must come to meals from now on and go to the outhouse during the day. Besides, it's better for Beth to be with us more so she gets to know us." Hal held her breath and waited.

"All right," Annie said evenly and left.

Hal took Redbird out to the garden with her to tell Emma they could set an extra plate at the table. Emma had a hand full of radishes by their leafy tops and was only half way down the row. "That is gute."

"From now on work in tasks for Annie to do that will keep her downstairs. Don't do anything for her that she should be doing herself," Hal said.

Emma smiled. "Jah, I understand."

That first dinner was the most awkward for Annie. Hal didn't get around to telling John and the boys Annie would be eating with them from now on. John's eyebrows shot up at Hal when Annie appeared and placed her baby's cradle on the floor by her chair.

Noah and Daniel eyed the girl until time for the silent prayer. After that nothing was more important than filling their plates with food. Hal tried to draw Annie into the conversation and received one or two word answers. Finally, the boys took over. By the time they explained what they had done that morning and talked about the animals, Annie was asking them questions.

After lunch, Hal said, "Annie, you can help Emma with clean up. I'm going to churn butter."

Annie nodded. Once she hadhelped Emma stack the dishes, Emma handed Annie a dish towel. While she washed, Emma asked, "Annie, can you sew on a treadle sewing machine?"

"I sew by hand. We did not own a sewing machine," Annie said as she set a dried plate on the stack.

"I remember those days. After Hallie had to sew a few clothes for herself by hand, she went looking for a sewing machine. I want to show you how to sew on our machine. It is so much faster than by hand. I really like using it. We have material for you to make another dress and apron, and you need more clothes for Beth. I can help you cut out the pieces and get you started," Emma told her.

"When am I to do this?" Annie asked.

"This afternoon is gute. Once I get you started I can make bread. If you have a question, just call for me," Emma said as she washed off the table. She walked around Hal sitting in a chair with the churn between her legs. When she glanced down, Hal winked at her.

After supper, Annie didn't have to be told to help with dishes. She stacked the dishes and carried them to the counter. "Tonight I can wash," she said timidly.

"Sounds gute to me," Emma said, smiling at her. "I like trading off."

In the living room, Hal went to the basket of mending and picked out a pair of Daniel's pants that needed a knee fixed. While she mended, she listened to the girls in the kitchen, getting aquainted and sounding more like sisters as time went by.

The next few days went smoothly. Annie came for meals and helped with kitchen cleanup. As long as she had something to sew on, she stayed downstairs in the afternoon. After supper clean up, Annie left quickly for her room with her baby.

One evening as they finished the dishes, Emma asked, "Have you ever been to school, Annie?"

"Nah, Papa did not think learning from books was necessary so none of us went to school," Annie said.

"Would you like to learn how to write your name and to read books?" Emma asked.

Annie said, "To have some education es a voonderball gute thing. I would like to be able to read books and write down things very much."

"Gute. I will give you some lessons," Emma said.

When the girls came into the living room, Emma said to Noah and Daniel, "Put away that checker board. We are having school tonight."

John peered at Hal over the top of his bible and gave her one of the many amazed looks she'd seen on his face lately. Hal smiled and went back to work, sewing a snap on Noah's jacket.

On in between Sunday afternoon, Elton and Jane Bontrager dropped by to visit. When they drove up, Annie, with an apprehensive look about her, grabbed Beth's cradle and headed for the stairs.

Hal stopped her. "Annie, come back here. The bishop and his wife will expect you to be here with us when they come to visit. They know you are a part of this family now. Sit down by Emma on the couch and act like it."

Annie did as she was told. John and Hal met the Bontragers at the door. Noah brought chairs from the kitchen for Jane and Elton. Annie kept her head down and clutched her baby to her.

Once they were seated, Hal said, "I don't believe you have met the newest members of our family. This is Annie Hosteller and her baby Beth."

Annie looked at them shyly and waited for their reactions.

"Gute to meet you, Annie," Jane said, giving her a friendly smile.

"Jah, we are glad you have found a home here. You could not have a better family to live with than John and Hallie Lapp and these children," Elton said warmly.

Annie nodded and said quietly, "I like it here."

"I baked three rhubarb pies this morning just encase we had company this afternoon," Emma said suggestively.

Elton leveled a long face at her. He said dolefully, "Jane has not baked me any such pie yet. Do I count as company?"

"That is why I mentioned it, Elton. Come, Annie. You can help me dish the pie up and serve it," Emma said, headed for the kitchen.

"Elton Bontrager, you make me out to be lazy. Our rhubarb

is not as early as the Lapp's plants. I will make you a pie as soon as I can," Jane scolded playfully, causing everyone to laugh.

As soon as the pie was devoured, Emma pulled Annie aside. "While the others visit, we have time to work on your schooling before supper."

The girls sat down at the living room table and quietly went to work on the alphabet and printing Annie's name.

John asked Elton the same question twice and gave up when he didn't answer. Elton was watching Emma instruct Annie. He turned to John and asked, "What are the girls doing?"

"Emma is teaching Annie to read and write."

Elton leaned forward and listened for a few minutes more. "Emma is a gute teacher. John, our teacher has told me she will not teach next fall. She is getting married. Would Emma take the job?"

John sounded amazed. "Emma teach?" He paused. "That is her decision to make. You should ask her."

Elton said, "I think I will before we leave."

In a little while, Annie said she was tired. Emma agreed they had worked long enough and complimented Annie on being a fast learner. She laid the pads and pencils on the shelf with the games.

Elton called to Emma, "Come talk to me before we go home. I have something to ask you."

Emma pulled a chair into the circle. Anna picked up her baby cradle and moved over by the sewing machine so she would be away from the group.

Emma asked, "What do you want to know, Elton?"

"We are in need of a teacher this fall. Would you be our new teacher?"

Emma gasped. "Teacher? I do not think I can be a teacher."

"You can. We have watched you work with Annie. We know you can," Elton assured her.

Emma gave him a doubtful look. "But that is one person not a class room full of children. I am not sure."

"Do not be so quick to turn me down. Give it some thought this week and let me know at the church meeting next Sunday. If you say nah, I can look else where," Elton said.

For the next few days, Hal didn't pressure Emma about becoming the teacher. She expressed once that she thought it would be a great opportunity for her. Emma didn't comment.

One morning, Hal, Emma and Annie shelled peas at the table. Emma hadn't said one word about what she was going to tell Elton on church Sunday. Hal's curiosity got the better of her. She had to know. "How are you coming with your decision for Elton about teaching?"

"I have not decided," Emma said.

"Sunday will be here all too quickly," Hal warned.

Emma said, "I just have never thought of myself as a teacher. I do not know if I would be gute at it."

Annie's head flew up. "You are very gute at it."

"I agree with Annie," Hal affirmed.

"My ability is not the only reason I hesitate," Emma said quietly.

"Tell us what you're thinking," Hal encouraged.

"I would be gone all day. You would be left to cook and do all the chores that I do along with your nursing duties. This would be a burden on you," Emma said.

"Is that your only excuse? Tell me this, would you like to be the teacher?" Hal insisted.

"The job would be a challenge, but maybe I would like to try it if things were different. It is just that I feel I am needed here more," Emma said in a noncommittal way.

"If you want that job, you tell Elton jah. I will do my very best to keep up," Hal assured her.

Annie had been looking from one to the other. "Can I say something?"

"Sure," Hal said.

"Nurse Hal, you do not have to work by yourself. I can help you do Emma's jobs so she can teach," Annie volunteered.

"There you go, Emma. Annie and I will have this all planned

out with some help from you, of course, on how to manage on our own come fall," Hal said eagerly.

"Annie, are you sure about this?" Emma asked.

"I am sure. You tell me I am part of this family. I should pitch in to help with the work. I tell you this family is very proud that the bishop picked you for the teacher. You should say jah," Annie insisted.

It was after that discussion that Emma worked with Hal and Annie so they could do many of the things she'd done. Hal wasn't sure Emma had much confidence in her when it came to cooking, but Annie was a quick study at anything. Hal had no doubts that between the two of them they would keep the household tasks done while Emma taught school.

Chapter 10

There was another hurtle that Annie had to brave. The timid girl still didn't go outside except to the outhouse and back as fast as she could. Hal wanted Annie to work with her outside as well as in. The girl could hoe in the garden, fed chickens, gather eggs and hang clothes on the line for starters.

One morning when it was finally shirt sleeve weather, Hal thought about a picnic at the picnic grove, It would be the first since last summer and might be just the thing to give Annie the courage to enjoy being outside.

Hal was helping snap green beans when she announced, "Emma, we're going to have a picnic in the walnut grove. Annie has been doing so gute in the house. Now we have to get her used to being outside. As long as those awful men are in jail she will be safe in our grove. Maybe she can fish in the pond with you and the boys."

"Might work," Emma agreed.

"At church Sunday, I want to invite the Keim family to come. How does next Wednesday sound for the picnic?"

Emma dropped a narrowed gaze at Hal. "Any certain reason you want to invite the Keims?"

Hal smiled from ear to ear. "I feel like doing some match

making. You watch Bobby and Annie when they're together. You'll see why."

Early the morning of the picnic, Hal started gathering up food to take with them. "I can hardly wait to get to the walnut grove. Are you ready, Annie?"

"Nah, I will not go," Annie said stubbornly, hanging the dish towel on the bar.

Emma said, "You will like the picnic once you get there."

Annie shook her head no.

"Annie," Hal breathed out slowly. "You have to be strong enough to make an effort. This house has become a prison. You can't allow those awful men to do that to you and ruin the rest of your life. You have to take the first steps back to the living, and the rest will follow easily. If you stay afraid to face life you'll never learn how to enjoy living. Tell you what. Let's start with a tour of the farm just to get you outside the fresh air and sunshine. We'll see how that goes."

"That is a gute idea," Emma said to Annie. "I have wanted you to see my chickens for a long time. You need to start gathering eggs to help Hallie while I teach."

"All right, if I must," Annie said reluctantly.

"Don't make it sound like I'm going to give you a dose of bad tasting medicine. Come along, girl," Hal said, motioning toward the door.

"Right now?"

"Jah, while the babies are napping is the best time. We have to call Noah and Daniel. They will want to show you the things that interest them," Hal told her.

Once out the door, Annie turned around in a circle, taking in the back yard. The martin apartment houses were full. The birds twittered to each other when Hal and Annie came close to the pole. The purple clematis vine, attached to the pole, was budded. Soon the woody vines would be covered with as many large flowers as leaves. Patches of rhubarb, asparagus and winter onions bordered the field fence. A few of the chickens lingered by the hen house, drinking from half a rubber car tire.

Annie said, "This is a peaceful place, your back yard."

When they were grouped together, Daniel insisted the tour begin with Tom Turkey.

"I have watched your turkey from the bedroom window. He is an interesting looking fellow," Annie said.

They moved to the coop. Daniel opened the door. The fretting hen burst out with her large family scattering around her feet. When she realized humans were near her, the hen bristled up and clucked furiously at her chicks to beware.

Daniel laughed. "That hen is telling her chicks to keep up with her so she can protect them, or one of us will catch them and eat them for dinner."

Last out of the coop was Tom. He followed the chicks, but at his own slow speed. With his neck stretched as long as he could make it, he eyed the Lapp family curiously.

"Gute morning, Tom," Daniel greeted.

The tiny turkey stopped and turned toward the direction of Daniel's voice. He moved his head one way than the other as he focused on Daniel. When Tom spotted the boy, he gave out a low nasal twang as a return greeting. Daniel threw a handful of cracked corn down in front of him. "Eat your breakfast, Tom, before the others get it."

Tom purred his thanks, and quickly pecked here and there in the grass. It didn't take long for him to finish off the corn. Tom chirped louder, letting it be known he wanted more to eat. Daniel squatted. Tom strutted to him and pecked Daniel's knee gently. "No more to eat until you speak for me. Say gobble, gobble, Tom."

The turkey stood very still, listening to the boy. Daniel raised his voice, "Go ahead. Show Annie you can speak. Say gobble, gobble."

Tom stretched his neck and gave a very loud, "Gobble, gobble." The little turkey patted one foot up and down on the ground and strutted in a circle as he fanned his tiny tail.

"Oh, how sweet he is," Annie said. "Tom understands what you say to him, Daniel. I have never heard of anyone making a pet out of a turkey." A cloud passed over her face. "What will happen to him when he grows up?"

Daniel looked uncertainly at Hal. "I have not thought of that."

"Tom is your pet. That means it is your decision as to what happens to him," Hal said.

Daniel thought a minute. "He is going to live on our farm forever and talk to everyone who wants to listen."

"Now that we have settled Tom's fate, I want to show you my chickens." Emma said causally without looking at Annie, "I let them out early on pretty days so they have already scattered this morning, but a few are on the nests laying." Inside the hen house, a hen crackled loudly to announce she'd laid an egg. Just as Emma and Annie reached the door, the excited hen flew out in front of them. "Peek in at the chicken nests. You gather the eggs later in the afternoon. The boys can show you where the corn is kept for the chicken's morning feeding. I open the door so they can be outside as much as possible and throw the corn on the ground.

About dark, the setting hen always takes her family back in the coop to roost. The hen house door needs shut and the coop, too, so the coons and possums will not get in. You can do that if you want to." Emma pointed out her new rooster, coming on the run when he heard her voice. "This proud cock is Abraham. He moves fast and will follow you around, but he will not hurt you. He is just looking for food and attention."

"Why did you pick that name?" Hal asked.

Emma chuckled. "Abraham in the bible lived to be a very old man. Maybe that name will help my rooster be lucky enough to live a long life."

Noah said, "Now it is my turn. I want to show Annie the barn."

He led them between the pens to show Annie a new litter of kittens, five all yellow and white and a black one. They were all in a row, sucking on a white cat. Noah picked a spitting, hissing kitten up and handed it to Annie. She laughed. "So much protest coming from such a tiny fuzz ball. This baby wants to be back with his mother," she said, handing the kitten to Noah.

As Noah showed Annie the milk parlor, Buttercat, scrambled down from the hay mow and walked slowly toward them with his tail twitching high in the air. "Meet Buttercat. He is the boss of all the cats in the barn. We have had him for a long time."

Annie watched him. "He seems to be very proud of his place in life."

Buttercat twisted his head up to look at Annie as if he understood her and rubbed in a circle around her legs as he purred.

"That is enough attention for Buttercat," Noah said. "Now come outside and see our cattle and horses."

The boys climbed the fence, straddled the top board and wrapped their bare feet over the middle board. The women looked over the fence as Noah pointed across the pasture at the cattle and horses, grazing.

Hal nodded toward the stand of trees on the far side the pasture. "That is the picnic grove. You can see it's way back from the road and dense enough that travelers can't see through the trees."

Annie nodded agreement. Trying to change the subject, she pointed across the pasture. "That is a nice pond. Your stock has plenty to drink."

"Noah said, "We like to fish in that pond. Do you like to fish?"

"I do not know. I have never fished before. I do not know how," Annie said.

Daniel jumped down by her. "We can teach you. You will find it fun once you do it."

"Jah," Noah agreed, "Fishing is easy."

"Maybe so. Now I have to feed Beth," Annie said softly and returned to the house.

Hal and Emma were busy packing picnic supplies into dish towel bundles when John came back from checking his lower pasture fence. "How did you make out with Annie? Is she coming to the picnic?"

"She did enjoy the tour we gave her, but I don't know if she's going with us. She wanted to say no. We just have to wait and see," Hal said.

Emma heard the crunch of rocks under moving wheels. She peered over the window half curtain. "Bishop Bontrager is here."

"John invite him in and tell him he should go get Jane and come to the picnic," Hal said.

In a few minutes, John and Elton came to find Hal in the kitchen. "Gute morning, Hal and Emma," Elton greeted.

"Gute morning, Elton. How about it? Want to go on a picnic and fish with the boys today?" Hal asked.

Elton had a dolorous look on his face. "Nah, not today."

Hal felt uneasy the moment she saw his expression, but she pressed on, "We're hoping that Annie will join us. It's time she traded this house for a breath of fresh air and some fun. It would do her gute to spend more time outside. Maybe we can all breathe easier now that the Hostellers are in jail."

Elton replied solemnly, "He who lives on maybes has a slender diet. The sheriff came to see me. He wanted to warn me to be prepared. The Hosteller men bonded out of jail."

Hal dropped the coffee pot on the table. "That's awful. John, what about our picnic?"

"Go ahead and have it. We do not have to tell Annie this news yet. She is safe enough here with all of us around her, and her father does not know she is with us."

"I feel like I'm deceiving her," Hal said miserably.

Right after Elton left, the Keim family showed up. Lovina and Bobby came inside while Adam waited on the porch steps.

Lovina laid a dishtowel bundle on the table. "This is fresh bread. Anything I can do to help?"

"Plenty. Help us pack all these bundles out the back door to the wagon," Emma suggested.

Bobby glanced around. "Is Annie coming?"

"Your guess is as good as mine," Hal said. "So far she hasn't said she would. Right now she's hiding in her bedroom."

"Can I go talk to her?" Bobby offered.

"Jah, give it a try," Hal said.

In a few minutes, Annie came down the stairs. Behind her was Bobby, carrying the baby.

Emma whispered to Hal, "Wonder how he managed that?"

"It's hard to explain, but keep your eyes on those two. I think you'll find the answer is a simple one," Hal replied, smiling.

Emma suggested, "Annie, we have a few food bundles left to carry out and stack in the wagon. Want to grab one?"

Adam tugged on the small red wagon's tongue while the women followed him down the lane between the fields. Way ahead of them, the others, poles and bait cans in hand, headed across the pasture.

"Adam, we never turn down gute help," Hal said. "But when we get to the picnic grove, you hurry along to the pond. You might be the lucky one today that gets us a mess of fish."

Adam nodded agreement and gave Hal a large smile.

The fresh country breeze gently buffed Hal's face. She took a deep breath and thanked God that her home was in the country. She watched Annie trudge timidly along beside her and anger for the Hosteller men rose in her. How could they have treated this sweet girl the way they did?

"Listen, Redbird," Hal said softly as she held the baby up in front of her. "Hear that mourning dove call? Right away another one will answer."

Annie waited until after the answering call to speak. "They aways sound so lonesome." She snuggled her baby up against her so she could pat Beth's back.

"Guess that is why they are called mourning doves," Lovina answered.

They went through the gate hole, and Hal stopped to pull the wire gate back to the fence post and secure it so the cows and horses wouldn't get out.

"Bobwhite. Bobwhite," whistled a quail. The wagon wheels

squeaked over the unlevel ground as Adam and the women walked too close to the covey. The quails burst from the tall grass nearby and flew low over the pasture, hunting a less crowded place to hide.

Cardinals flew back and forth from the cedar trees, disappearing into their nests in the thick boughs. That was a safe, dense cover in which to raise their babies.

Hal took the wagon handle from Adam and pointed toward the pond. As he took off on the run, Hal led the others past the outer line of walnut trees, filled with singing birds. She said to Annie, "We pick blackberries from that thicket in July and pick up walnuts in late fall." They walked into the clearing. Hal looked around. "Not much clutter is there? Watch where you walk though. The cows have been in here and not every pile is dry. I appreciate they keep the grass clipped short, but what goes in one end comes out the other." That brought a laugh from Lovina and Emma and even Annie chuckled.

The women scathered out to pick up fallen limbs to pile a fairly high stack for the fire.

Emma dropped an armload of sticks. "This stack should be large enough to roast hot dogs and marshmallows," she said. "I am going fishing now."

"Go. Enjoy," Hal said, waving her away.

Holding out her arms to Hal, Lovina asked, "Can I hold Redbird? I'd like to get acquainted?"

Hal handed the baby over. She struck a match on a rock and dropped it in a small pile of dried leaves under the edge of the sticks. She watched the flames grow stronger before she went to the wagon for the bundles.

"Bless her. That girl is afraid to go enjoy herself," Lovina said softly, clucking her tongue against her teeth.

Hal looked where Lovina nodded. She walked over to Annie, peeking out of the trees and held out her arms. "Lovina is holding Redbird so give me Beth. Go on and fish with the others. It's just a suggestion, but if I were you I'd sit by Bobby and let him teach you to fish. He cares a lot about you."

110

Annie's eyes widened. "Did he say that?"

"Nah, but I can see it in his eyes," Hal shared.

Annie left the cover of the trees. As if she were a rabbit sniffing for danger, Annie walked a few feet then stopped. She stared around her long enough to feel less nervous and continued on. When she reached Bobby, Hal couldn't make out the conversation, but she saw the young man point over his shoulder.

Annie picked up a pole out of the grass, baited it and sat down by Bobby. They didn't say much, but Hal had the feeling they weren't exactly oblivious of each other if the way they darted glances back and forth was any indication.

Hal hadn't realized Lovina slipped up behind her and was watching, too. "Nurse Hal, spring is truly a season of rebirth. Love and dreams of love begin in this season. Watch Bobby and Annie."

Hal agreed, "I believe you're right. Do you mind that Bobby is interested in Annie? After all, she is unmarried and does have a baby by questionable parentage."

"Who Bobby chooses is his decision. I feel sorry for Annie. She has been through so much that was not of her doing. With the right husband, she could be a gute wife. As for her baby, that little one would never have to know any other father than the one that is married to her mother. That is how I feel," Lovina said firmly.

"That is how I feel as well," Hal affirmed. "We treat Annie as if she is one of the family. We've told her she and the baby can live with us as long as she wants to."

"You are gute and kind. Your love will make a difference in the way Annie gets over all that happened to her," Lovina said. "The fire is blazing pretty gute. Suppose we should call them all to dinner now?"

"Jah, it is time. They have all afternoon to fish," Hal cupped her hands around her mouth and shouted, "Dinner is ready. Calling all fishermen. Come eat."

As they ate their roasted hot dogs, pork n beans and potato

chips, the fishermen grumbled that fish hadn't been biting all morning. They hoped the afternoon would be luckier. After they ate, they wandered back down to the pond and scattered around the bank. Only Bobby and Annie sat close together.

A deer fly buzzed past Annie's face and tried to light in her hair. She slapped at the fly, but the insect was persistent. It kept buzzing around her close enough to give her cold chills. It dodged her batting hand and came right back.

"That fly can not take nah for an answer," Bobby said. "It has been bothering me, too. Sooner or later one of us will not miss."

Annie didn't reply. She was listening to tiny ripples slap the pond bank. What a peaceful, soothing sound that was.

Bobby raised his arm to brush away a small trickle of perspiration off his cheek. "That sun has some power in it this afternoon. I am getting warm."

Annie concentrated on her bobber in the water. A swarm of water spiders collided with it. A slivery blue dragonfly hovered over her line, made another pass and flew too close, hit the line and flew away. A frog came out of the muddy bank from behind a rock and jumped into the pond with a loud splat. Annie thought the frog making that noise would scare the fish away.

Bobby tapped Annie's hand and got a sharp look for his trouble. "Funny thing, ain't?" He asked as he went back to watching his bobber.

"What is so funny?"

"I was sure I had a pretty girl sitting beside me, but I've been talking to myself I guess." His lips twitched as he tried not to grin.

She blushed, embarrassed by the compliment. "You know I am right here. I did not think you said anything that deserved an answer."

Bobby laid his fishing pole beside him and stretched out in the grass. He put his hands behind his head. With eyes half shut, he said lazily, "Reckon if I was to say you just caught a fish that would not be of importance to you, either."

"I did?" Annie asked, directing her attention back to her bobber. The red and white bobber danced and zig zagged in the water. "What do I do now?"

"Turn that crank on the reel to bring the fish in, and we will see what you caught," Bobby said.

Annie cranked as fast as she could while Bobby leaned up on his elbow to watch. Annie gave a jerk and out of the water flew a small silver bluegill. The fish landed on Bobby's face and flip flopped to the grass. "I caught a fish. My first fish. What do I do with him?"

Bobby laughed as he grabbed the line above the struggling fish and held it away from him. "One thing you do not do is throw your fish at my mouth. I like to eat my fish fried."

Annie quailed at Bobby's teasing. "I'm sorry. I can not imagine what you must think of me?"

Bobby wanted to say he was sorry he upset her. With all she had been through in her short life, he understood how she had trouble relating to other people that only wanted to be kind to her. He knew so well what she was feeling. He'd seen people teased Adam. He'd come to Adam's rescue plenty of times. Then again, last thing Annie needed was to feel sorry for herself. She had to learn to stand on her own two feet and take a little teasing.

"Quite One, you want to know what I think of you. I will tell you," he said softly. "I think you are the shiest, quietest girl I have ever met. One that needs all the friends she can get. I want to be one of those friends if you will let me."

This time Annie had been looking right at Bobby while he spoke until she heard the rolling wheels of a buggy pull to a stop on the road. When she glanced that direction, her face turned deathly pale. She cried out. The enclosed buggy door opened, and her father stared across the pasture at her.

She was frozen with terror. Bobby saw her reaction and recognized her father. "How did he get out of jail?"

Annie whispered hoarsely, "I do not know, but he will be

113

here soon to get me."

"Nah, I do not think the Sheriff will let him take you," Bobby assured her.

In a choked voice, Annie said, "My father will not ask. That is not his way. I am going back to the picnic grove and get my baby. I want to go to my room now." She threw down her fish pole and took off on a run to the trees.

"I will go with you," Bobby said as he followed Annie to the picnic grove.

Chapter 11

When Annie came back to the edge of the trees the buggy was gone. She clutched her baby to her and ran so fast to the house that the others couldn't keep up with her. She sat down on the couch to catch her breath until everyone joined her. She was shaking like maple tree leaves blowing in a stiff breeze.

Hal assured her, "You're safe, Annie."

Annie clasped her trembling hands together to still them, but that didn't help. "I wish I did not feel so afraid. Look at my hands. I do not know if they will ever stop shaking." Anne's face was colorless as she rambled, "Nurse Hal, now they know I am here. Somehow, my father has gotten out of jail. He was on the road, watching me at the pond. You are all in danger now. They will come for me. I know they will."

"I didn't mean for this to happen. We knew the Hosteller men had bonded out, but I didn't want to spoil your day," Hal confessed.

"You should have told me. I should have stayed in the house in my room where he could not see me. None of you will be safe as long as my father and brothers are free," Annie cried. "This very night they will come for me."

"Not without a fight from us," Hal told her.

115

John declared, "We will be with you, Annie, all the time from now on."

After the Keims left, John propped his hunting rifle by the front door again. Noah put his hunting rifle by the back door. Hal carried her broom and the mop into the clinic room. She leaned them up against the wall.

John asked, "What are those for?"

"I killed a mouse with this broom. I can clobber a two legged rat with it if I have to," Hal stated.

Emma said, "The mop is mine."

None of them felt like talking that evening. Their ears were tuned in to what was happening beyond the house walls. Each time they heard a buggy passing, they tensed and held their breaths until the buggy went on by.

Daniel and Noah tried to play a game of Scrabble, but their minds weren't on it. Daniel broke the silence when he announced, "We need a dog. One that barks when someone is coming in."

"That idea is too late to do us any gute right now," John said.

Hal added, "I agree with Daniel. We should get a dog."

"All right," John agreed and went back to reading the newspaper, The Budget.

After they turned in for the night, Hal couldn't get to sleep. She heard every creak and groan the old house made. Outside, the animals seemed restless. However, maybe they always called to each other in the night, and she just hadn't stayed awake to listen.

Late that night, wheels of a buggy turn into the driveway. When the turning wheels stopped, a horse behind the barn whinnied. A horse so close it seemed to be in front of the house answered back.

Hal woke up John. "Someone is in the yard. I'm sure of it."

John slipped into his pants and pattered barefoot down the hall to the stairs. "Wake the boys. I will go look."

Hal patted Noah then Daniel on the shoulder. "Wake up. Someone is outside."

She glided into Emma's room. "Emma, be prepared. I heard a buggy come in."

Last was Annie's room. "Annie, someone is outside."

"They have come for me and my baby," the girl said, grasping Hal's hand.

"They won't be coming upstairs. We won't let them." Hal laid her baby down beside Beth. "Here, you take care of Redbird for me. Stay in your room until we tell you it's safe to come out."

John peeked out the living room window, watching for movement. Noah pointed his rifle at the mud room door. Daniel was behind the door with the baseball bat. Hal and Emma made a fast trip to the clinic and grabbed their weapons, ready to defend the clinic door. Annie was stationed in her bedroom with her pepper spray to guard the babies.

"Emma, spray the mop rag with that pepper spray. That would be much more effective at discouraging a man attacking us if you're rubbing the mop in his face, but don't get it on me or you," Hal cautioned. She walked back to the clinic door. "John, what do you see?"

"No moon tonight. I can make out a buggy parked in the dark of the barn. Several men are spreading out to surround the house. Be prepared at all doors."

"We are," Hal replied on her way back to the clinic. She grabbed her nursing bag out of the cupboard and fumbled in it for her cell phone. She prayed that the battery was still charged.

"Hallie, what are you doing with that phone? We do not need medical help," Emma chastised. The amended with, "Yet."

"Nah, but hopefully some of the men sneaking up on us will," Hal said as she dialed 911. "This is John Lapp's wife, Hallie, on 60th Street. We need help out here right away. The house is surrounded by the Hosteller men. They intend to harm us."

"Help will be on the way," the dispatcher said. "How many are there?"

"Six or seven maybe," Hal said and hung up.

Emma whispered, "How do you know how many men are out there?"

"I don't. Six or seven sounded gute enough to warrant plenty of help," Hal hissed.

Forceful bangs against the living room door gave them the idea someone was trying to kick their way in. When Daniel walked in his sleep John put thumb bolt locks on that door and the back one. Getting in wouldn't be easy but if the kicking continued the door would give. John yelled, "Stop that or I will shoot through the door."

After that Hal didn't have time to worry about John. Shoes sounded sharp and hard on the boards as men rushed across the porch and stopped in front of the clinic door. The knob twisted. The door burst open. Framed in the opening were two men.

"Look, James, the Lapp women are waiting for us," Henry Hosteller sneered and laughed derisively.

"Leave now," Hal ordered raising the broom higher and brandishing it in the air.

James guffawed and slapped his thigh as he edged toward Emma. "Best news I've heard all day, Uncle Henry. Two women waiting for us."

Hal came down hard on the side of Henry's head with her broom. The impact was hard enough to snap his head into bouncing back and forth like a broken spring. Losing his balance, he crashed to the floor, holding his head. Before he came to his senses enough to get up, Hal sprayed his face with pepper spray. Henry screamed and rolled out the door.

At the same time, Emma rammed the business end of the pepper sprayed mop into James's face. The blow stopped the man in his tracks. His eyes filled with fury as he spewed a few cuss words. Then the pepper spray took effect, and he covered his face with his hands. He howled and back away with Emma hitting his hands with the mop all the way. Just outside the door, James bungled into the writhing Henry, tripped over his body and did a backward summer salt off the porch. Emma

118

slammed the door.

"Emma, guard this door while I check on everyone else," Hal said. She darted into the living room and found John holding Eli Hosteller at bay with his rifle. The man was stout enough to break in the door but decided he was no match for a gun.

A grunting noise came from the mud room. Hal ran there. Confronted with Noah and his rifle the teenage boy, Marvin, had stopped long enough for Daniel to whack him over the head with the ball bat. He was out cold.

Hal praised, "Gute job, boys. I'll watch him. Noah, go help Emma guard the clinic. Daniel, run upstairs and make sure Annie's all right. Tell her what's going on so she calms down."

Hal walked over to the counter and lifted the curtain with a finger to looked out. With a flood of relief, she saw strobe lights flashing on the glass. Help had arrived.

She heard a shuffling noise. She wheeled around. On the opposite side of the table, Marvin leered at her, opening and shutting his hands into fists. If looks could kill, she would soon be dead. She surely would be if Marvin ever got his hands on her. The boy edged warily around the table. She glanced toward the door, hoping someone would come to her aid.

"Do not say a word," Marvin hissed. "You had no business butting into a Hosteller matter. We will take Annie back where she belongs. If not tonight then sometime soon. You will not succeed."

He took another step forward with his fists doubled up. He intended to strike her. She didn't cringe as he was probably used to the women in the Hosteller compound doing. She lifted her broom up in the air menacingly to let him know she would fight and gave him her best defiant stare.

Rubbing his sore head, Marvin took a step backward as he eyed her. He gulped and his eyes shifted one way then the other as he tried to decide what to do next. This wasn't the way a confrontation with a woman was supposed to go. At home, they cowered down and never fought back.

"Annie has been through more than enough because of your family. She's staying right where she is. You're in enough trouble without making more for yourself. Sheriff deputies are outside now to take you and the others to jail. Don't try anything else. There are as many lawman out there as fleas on that mangy, starved dog of Joseph's," Hal warned him.

Marvin's eyes widened as he heard the deputies rough voices. One on the porch ordered, "Lay face down and put your hands on your head." A deputy in the yard ordered a man to put down his club or he'd be shot. Hurried steps of several other lawmen pounded up the porch steps. Two of them plastered themselves on both sides the broken door. A voice shouted, "Deputy sheriff Johnson."

John said, "Come on in."

Shifting from one foot to the other, Marvin gulped again. He didn't like the situation he was in even a little bit. He could over power Hal and make her sorry for meddling in his family business, but the law was going to burst through the kitchen door any second. He didn't want arrested again. Marvin back away from Hal, turned and ran out the back door.

Hal leaned against the counter, afraid that her shaking knees would give way just as a deputy filled the doorway with a gun in his hand.

"Don't shoot," Hal said. "The only weapon I've got is this broom."

The deputy grinned. "Are you all right?"

"I am now. One of the younger Hosteller men just ran out the back door. His name is Marvin."

The deputy backed up and shouted across the living room. "Anyone free enough to go after one that got away come with me to the back of the house."

"Three other uniformed men raced out the back door behind the deputy. It wasn't long before they returned. In the dark with so many places to hide, they didn't spot him.

Hal joined John at the door to watch the Hosteller men loaded into the patrol cars. The tables had turned on them. This surprise assault by the Lapp family had taken the wind out of their sails.

A few days later, the sheriff stopped by after the Hosteller hearing to tell John the men would be held in jail this time until their trial without bond.

Annie had worked up a large amount of anger. She was fed up with the Hostellers. They tried to hurt her new family. "Sheriff, I would like to testify at the trial."

"Annie, are you sure?" Emma asked in amazement.

Annie shrugged fatalistically. "I want to do it."

"If my testimony will help, I can testify against them, too," Hal said. "I treated Nonnie Hosteller after she had been beaten and Annie."

"It sure will help to hear from you two ladies," the sheriff said. "I'll let the district attorney know."

Chapter 12

The century old district court house was too far away to take a buggy to it. Hal hired a van to transport Bobbie Keim, Annie and her. They arrived a little early that morning so they parked and waited.

Hal said to the driver, Abe Smothers, from Wickenburg. "You can come inside and watch if you want. It will be air conditioned in there."

"Sounds like a good idea," he agreed.

Bobby said, "Come on with me, Abe. I will go in and save two seats so Hal and Annie do not have to come in until the last minute.

After the men went into the courthouse, the prisoner van pulled up. As the Hosteller men walked down the sidewalk, Joseph was in the lead with the other men trailing along behind like dogs heeling their master.

Reporters line up on both sides of the sidewalk, waiting for Joseph Hosteller to walk by. One reporter yelled at the old man, asking him if he had anything to say.

Joseph glared back and said sourly, "The Amish should be ashamed of themselves to treat us, their own kind, this way. They changed the rules and expected us to obey them. They tried to force their laws on us and expected us to like them. We will not do that ever. None of my men will talk to you. This is all we have to say."

Once the prisoners disappeared through the double doors, Hal and Annie walked down the sidewalk. Before they reached the gauntlet of reporters, Hal saw Phil King perk up at the sight of her. When he recognized her, he stretched his neck out like Daniel's turkey, ready to attack any moving object.

When Hal got even with King she put her arm around Annie's shoulders to shield her. Phil King, brash as always, stepped in front of the girl. He spoke loudly for the other reporters to hear. "My name is Phil King, reporter for the Wickenburg News. Can I get you to give me a statement for my newspaper, Miss? Are you Annie Hosteller? Anything to say about the charges against your family? Give me your thoughts for the newspaper, will you?"

Annie wilted as close beside Hal as she could get and still walk. She glanced from under her bent head apprehensively at Phil King and at the surroundings.

Stepping out around the reporter, Hal retorted as she walked, "Phil, you grew up in this town. You know as well as I do what this is doing to the Amish community. They have a modest lifestyle and are deeply religious, gentle people that like to live in peace. This ordeal is very upsetting to all of them. They are born to live peaceful, quiet ways and forgive others. For anymore you'll have to come inside and listen."

The other reporters along the sidewalk had taken notes. Now they all burst out with questions at the same time. Hal said, "We haven't anymore to say." She walked briskly the few feet to the courthouse's double doors, pulling the girl with her.

Inside, people talked in low murmurs. This trial had drawn a large crowd. It wasn't often that they were witness to Amish people in court. Hal looked behind her. The reporters were filing in and taking up the back rows. Bobby waved to get their attention. He was up close to the front with two empty seats. Hal made Annie go in first to sit next to Bobby.

Annie whispered, "I do not think I can do this. My insides are trembling. I feel sick. Maybe I am going to throw up."

"It's nerves. I feel the same way. Just keep telling yourself you are freeing you and your daughter. You will make it through this," Hal said. "When you're on the stand, look at me as if you're talking to me. That will help get you through the testifying." She checked out the jury and found she didn't recognize any of the four women and eight men. Too bad there hadn't been more women picked for the jury. Deliberation wouldn't have taken long once she and Annie talked about how the Hosteller men treated women. Of course, Hal figured the lawyer for the defense had that same thought.

In a few minutes, the clerk of court stood up in front and said loudly, "Court is now in session. All rise. The honorable Sara Shriver presiding."

Voices stilled, and a soft rustle of clothes could be heard as people stood. A woman, in her forties, stepped into the courtroom from a side door. Sleek shoulder length, straight, blond hair framed her slim face and the billowing black robe draped around her slender frame. As soon as she was sat down, the clerk of court said, "Be seated."

"Now first thing I want to do is speak to the press," the judge said as she scanned the back row. "You are all aware that this trial involves Amish people from our community. We are going to respect their rights and beliefs during this legal procedure. That means no cameras are allowed in this court. Amish people do not want their pictures taken. That is their right. This court intends to respect that right. For the reporters and spectators, I don't want to see cell phones in here. It would be too tempting to sneak a picture or interrupt the preceding with one of those terrible ring tones. Anyone caught disobeying my rules will be found in contempt of court and banned from the rest of the trial. Now we may precede with opening statements."

The opening statements didn't take too long. Both lawyers seemed to be in a hurry to get to the witnesses. Bobby Keim was called to the stand and sworn in. The district prosecutor,

Warren Mutton, was middle aged with a spreading middle. He told Bobby to say in his own word what happened. Bobby told how the Hosteller men had burst into his family's house in the middle of the night. They beat him until he could hardly stand, looking for Joseph Hosteller's daughter. Bobby said his mother had been ill for some time. The invasion was very upsetting to her and to his younger brother.

The Hosteller defense attorney, William Curtis, was neatly dressed in a black suit. Hal heard he was from Bloomfield. He stood up and asked if Bobby had any proof to show that the intrusion took place. Bobby replied he did. He drove himself to the Amish medical clinic and was checked over by Nurse Hal Lapp. All the Lapp family was present at the time and saw the shape he was in after the beating.

"During the attack that you alleged happened, did you see Joseph Hosteller?"

"Nah, but his sons -----." Bobby was cut off.

"No further questions. Your witness."

The district attorney said, "I haven't anymore questions at this time. I'd like to call Hallie Lapp to the stand."

Bobby stepped down. Annie grabbed Hal's hand and whispered, "If you need to stay strong just look at me."

Hal winked at her and walked up front. After she was sworn in, district attorney Dutton came to stand by her. "Will you please tell the court what happened on your first meeting with the Hostellers?"

Hal told she had gone to the Keim house for a medical need. On the way home, she was pulled off the road by five Hosteller men. Joseph Hosteller demanded that she treat his sick wife and led her horse to his house. Hal described Nonnie Hosteller's wounds.

Dutton asked, "In your opinion was Joseph Hosteller's wife beaten?"

"Objection. That is a leading question," shouted the defense lawyer.

"Sustained," the judge ruled.

The prosecuting attorney said, "What did you find as a cause for Mrs. Hosteller's injuries?"

"In my opinion as a nurse, she had been beaten," Hal said.

Defense lawyer Curtis shot out of his seat. "Objection. Hallie Lapp can't testify to that. She was not present when Mrs. Hosteller was injured."

Judge Shriver said, "I'll allow Mrs. Lapp her professional opinion."

Dutton said, "Tell us what made you think Nonnie Hosteller's injuries were more than a fall."

"I've worked for many years in Home Health Care with the elderly. One of the leading cause of injury in the elderly is falls. I based my findings for Mrs. Hosteller on what I've seen before. Her injuries weren't consistent with a fall. She had a cut and bruised cheek on the right side of her face, and her left wrist was broken. I made a point of asking her if she was right handed, and she said yes.

Now just think about it. If a person suddenly falls, usually that person puts out the dominate hand to stop the fall. She should have put out her right hand. Besides that, the injury to her face was on her right cheek. If she had landed on her left wrist which was broken, she'd have been falling to the left and had the bruise and cut on her left cheek not the right one."

"While you were at the Hosteller farm did you see anything that looked out of the ordinary to you?"

Hal darted a glance at the Hosteller men. They narrowed their eyes at her as if to scare her into not talking. "When I was leaving, I saw a man in a chicken house. He appeared just long enough at the window for me to notice him and ducked out of sight. The light from the window allowed me to see the door was barred from the outside. The man had been forced to live in there like an animal."

"Did anything else happen that was alarming to you?"

"Not that night but the next day, I was taking Lovina Keim to the doctor in my car. Her two sons, Bobby and Adam, went along. As we neared the Hosteller farm driveway, Henry

126

Hosteller raced down the driveway in a buggy."

"Why would he do that?"

"I don't know, but I felt like he meant to run me off the road which could have caused injury to me and my passengers. At the very least, I'd have wrecked my car. The Hostellers wanted me to be afraid of them so I wouldn't talk about Nonnie Hosteller's injuries to anyone."

"Did you think you have reason to fear them?"

"Yes, but I knew even more than Joseph Hosteller thought I did. His daughter, Annie, had been living with us. Actually hiding at our house to keep the Hosteller men from taking her home. She came to our house badly beaten by her father, Joesph. Through her we learned how horrible life was in the Hosteller community."

"No further questions. Your witness."

The defense attorney came forward. "Mrs. Lapp, did Nonnie Hosteller tell you her husband beat her?"

"No, she didn't. Her husband was ----."

"No further questions." He stated before she could finish and sat back down.

"You may step down," the judge said.

Clerk called, "Annie Hosteller to the stand"

Annie looked like a spooked deer as she moved forward with so many people watching her. She clasped her shaky hands together and prayed that she'd be able to make it though the questioning.

The district attorney began with, "Annie, life has been very difficult for you growing up in your father's house. Can you tell us about it?"

With a quiver in her quiet voice, Annie looked out to the seats at Hal and stated, "Since I was six years old, the men in the community have raped me."

"Did your father molest you?"

"Nah, but he left me to the mercy of my brothers and cousins. My father spent his time with the wives and daughters of the other men. He called laying down with them his way to cleanse them of the devil."

"You didn't report what happened to you to anyone?"

"The women were kept on the farm. None of us had any way of getting to someone that might help us, and we were too afraid to say anything if we had the chance. To disobey my father or brothers for any reason was cause for a bad beating.

The rapes on me started when I was a small child. Even then I knew we were a closed society. We did not go to English lawmen for anything. My father was our law."

"Did you tell your mother about the rapes?"

"Jah, I told her, they hurt me."

"What did she say?"

"She told me all I could do was pray hard for the men to stop raping me. When praying did not help, I told my mother again. She said I should fight to stop the men. That did not help. The men started coming as a group and held me down. They threw my skirt over my head so I could not see and took turns. I thought I would suffocate before they were each finished hurting me. While they were holding me down, they laughed and joked about my screaming and crying for them to stop." Annie put her hand over her mouth and choked on a sob.

The judge said, "Annie, would you like the questioning stopped for awhile so you can regain your composure?"

"Nah, I will finish now." She looked at the lawyer.

He said, "You're doing fine. Just take your time."

Annie took a deep breath and began, "When I was older, I tried once to talk to my father. He threatened that I could not tell a soul what happened in our community, or I would be punished. When I became pregnant, I had no way of knowing who the father was. My mother helped me deliver my baby girl the night before Nurse Hal stopped to care for my mother. While no one was looking, I hid my baby in her buggy. I could not stand to think of my baby growing up in the community and suffering like me and the other women. When my mother found the baby was gone she told my father. He asked me where the baby was. I said she died so I buried her, but he did not believe me. He had my brothers beat me, but I would not tell them where they baby was. I pretended to faint so they put me to bed. I heard them say they would start in on me again in the morning. Sooner or later, I would talk. So I slipped out in the night and ran to the Keim farm. The next morning, Bobby Keim took me to the Lapp farm, because he thought Nurse Hal should look me over."

"Tell me why did you wait until now to talk?"

For a second, Annie met her father's glowering stare and then she focused on Hal for courage. "As a child, I did not speak English. We used Pennsylvania Dutch. I did not have chances to be around a stranger that I could tell I needed help. One that could understand me. My father saw to that. He told me no one would believe me anyway. He said if I told I had been raped many times a stranger would say that was not rape. They would say I was asking for it."

"Why didn't your mother protect you?"

Without hesitation, Annie stated, "Fear and helplessness just like all the other women. My father beat her at least once almost ever day and more often when he was drunk. She did anything she could to stay on his gute side for her own sake. She said to me that I couldn't talk about what happened. All I could do was forgive the men. She even made me tell my father I forgave my brothers and cousins for hurting me. I guess she thought Papa might go easier on me. He didn't. I could not take any more. That's why I ran away. To find someone to tell. I prayed that my father was wrong. That someone would believe me and help me."

"Now you are willing to talk about this?"

Annie met her father's glaring eyes. "Jah, I am. I do not want the same kind of life for my daughter that I had."

Joesph Hosteller stood up and roared at the jury. "I believe God will forgive me for anything I have done."

Annie's face paled but she lifted her chin high. With more courage than she had ever shown before and without blinking, she exclaimed, "For the years you are in jail I hope you hear me screaming in your nightmares. You are my father. You should have protected me and not allowed those awful things to happen to me."

The district attorney said in his closing argument that Annie was imprisoned in her own home. She had lost her childhood because of the men on trial. She been brainwashed to keep her from talking against them.

As soon as the trial was about to adjourn for the day, Hal lead Bobby and Annie back to the van. She wanted to get away before the reporters circled them again. The driver drove them back to Bobby's buggy in the Wickenburg city parking lot.

It was a week later that the sheriff stopped by to tell the Lapp family the jury was not out very long. The verdict was guilty.

The Hosteller men each received ten years in prison. As a result of Annie's testimony, Nonnie Hosteller was charged with one count of failure to report a crime which was a misdemeanor. She was sentenced to 30 days in jail and two years probation.

The judge ordered that other agencies be called in to check on mistreatment of the Hosteller followers, arrange for education for the children and make the followers improved living conditions for the children.

Chapter 13

It was turning into one of those days without enough minutes in it. Hal and Annie washed laundry. After they had the clothes flapping on the line, they went to help Emma picked a bushel of green beans.

Hal heard one of the babies crying. She straightened up and braced her back to get the kinks out. "I'll go see which one of the babies is unhappy."

Annie turned an ear to the house. "It is Redbird."

"How can you tell?" Emma asked, throwing a handful of green beans into the basket.

"She has a different sounding cry from Beth," Annie said simply.

"Will you look there," Hal said. "What do you suppose that turkey is up to? He looks like he's headed on a mission."

The girls stood and watched as Tom strutted toward the barn.

Emma said, "He has taken to following Daniel around. When Daniel is out of his sight, Tom is lost. He follows the chickens."

Buttercat jumped up on the barn half door and plopped off on the ground right in a flock of hens. They squawked as they scattered. Tom stopped and stretched his neck to see what

131

frightened the chickens. When he spotted Buttercat walking proudly away from the barn, Tom stuck his head low and raced at the cat. He stopped, stomped a foot in warning and flew at Buttercat, planting his feet in the cat's face. Buttercat, taken by surprise, crouched down and squalled back. Tom bounced back at him again with his claws aimed at Buttercat's eyes.

"That turkey means business," Hal said. "Why is he acting that way?"

"Tom has gotten very protective of the chickens. They are his family," Emma said. "He came at me a few days ago when I stepped on one of the hens while I was feeding them."

"I can't let him beat up on Buttercat." Hal took off running to the fight. "Tom, shoo! Get away."

Tom turned to her voice and saw her apron waving at him. By the time he wheeled around to attack Buttercat again, the cat flashed out of sight. Tom decided he didn't have a reason to stick around. He strutted off toward the regathering chickens.

Later that morning, Hal got a call to go deliver Katie Bender's baby. She didn't know where the Bender farm was so she asked, "Emma, how about going with me? You need the practice."

"I do not think I can. We never know how long a birthing will take. I should be home snapping beans to can and fixing meals," Emma said.

Annie spoke up firmly, "It is a gute idea for Mama Hal to have you along until Marvin Hosteller is caught. I will snap the beans and do the cooking."

So Emma consented to go with Hal to deliver the Bender baby. The meal was an easy one. Emma had a lot of early preparations done. Not much to putting together vegetable soup to simmer while she snapped green beans. After dinner and clean up was over, Annie took the babies upstairs for a nap.

She laid down on the bed beside the infants to get them to go to sleep, and the next thing she knew she woke up from a sound sleep. For an instant, she laid very still, listening. Something woke her but what. She slipped out of bed and glided to the window. She scanned across the back yard and the road to the west. Nothing there.

A couple horses whinnied. One of them seemed close. A faint slap of the living room screen door sent fear through her. She leaned with her ear on the closed bedroom door and listened. There was subdued movement downstairs and whispering voices. Soft footsteps went from room to room. The sound of walking was louder as someone climbed up the stairs, moving cautiously.

Annie came away from the door. She picked up Redbird and gently laid her under the bed and then Beth. Both babies were sleeping soundly. Annie remade the bed, pulling the covers over the edge and to the floor as much as she could to hide the under side of the bed. She soft footed it over to the table and picked up her can of pepper spray. Then she laid down on the floor and bellied under the bed between the babies.

The bedroom door squeaked slowly open. Annie bit her top lip to keep from crying out and tried not to breathe. The noise woke the babies. Beth looked at her mother and smiled. Redbird wiggled and yawned. All too soon they would both decided to get vocal about wanting to eat. Annie stuck a finger in each baby's mouth to keep them busy. She hoped the men left soon. A dry finger wasn't going to be good enough to keep both babies quiet for very long.

"Marvin, this has been a wasted trip. I told you we would not find anyone home. Nurse Hal will not leave Annie here by herself as long as you are still around," a young man said in a low voice.

"Lester, I should have busted that nosy woman a good one when I had the chance," blustered Marvin as he smacked his fist in the palm of his other hand.

The pop made the babies grow wide eyed. Annie smiled at each of them to let them know they didn't need to be afraid.

"Keep your voice down. I want to get out of here before we get caught. So far I am not in trouble, but you are." Lester said, "Take my advice, if you do not want to go to jail you better get over the county line fast. Will not do you any good to get even now. Luck is on the Lapp family's side as far as Annie and that baby is concerned."

"Do not care a thing about that baby. Would just as soon wring its neck. Now Annie is a different story. Figured on taking her with me," Marvin sneered.

Annie laid her head between the babies and waited as the two men walked around the bed. One opened the storage closet door and closed it.

"The house is empty. Let's get out of here," Lester begged.

This time they didn't worry about making noise as they tromped down the stairs and slammed the front door. Annie stayed quiet for a moment, listening to the stillness.

"What are you doing in that house?" Yelled an angry voice from outside.

Annie jerked up so fast her head connected with a bed flat. That was Bobby Keim's voice. Why was he here? If he had only waited for a few more minutes Marvin and Lester would have been gone.

"Mind your own business," Marvin snarled back.

Annie couldn't hear what else they said. She knew Marvin. He was angry he didn't find her home. He would beat up Bobby with Lester's help just to take his anger out on someone. Anyone would do. Bobby didn't stand a chance against two of them. Being Amish, he probably wouldn't even try to fight back.

With up most care, Annie slipped out from under the bed. She wanted to make sure Bobby was all right, but she hated to leave the babies. All she could do was pray that one or both of them didn't cry out. The babies were safe enough hidden where they were. Bobby wasn't safe at all.

Annie went downstairs, listening as the angry words grew louder.

"I asked you what are you doing here," Bobby snapped.

Marvin replied harshly, "Looking for Annie."

"Did you hurt that girl?" Bobby demanded.

By then, Annie had made it to the living room window. She peeled back the curtain with one finger.

Marvin shook his head. "No one home."

"Until now," Lester said. "Nosy Bobby Keim is here now."

"He might be sorry he came to visit," Marvin said, clenching his fists as he moved toward Bobby.

Bobby stood his ground, watching Marvin advance. With Bobby's attention on Marvin, Lester circled around behind Bobby. Annie couldn't stand it. They were going to gang up on Bobby and hurt him. Maybe being Amish meant Bobby couldn't fight, but she could. As she started for the door, she spotted John's rifle against the wall. She picked it up and eased the door open just as Marvin punched Bobby on the jaw. Lester sidestepped, and Bobby went flying across the yard.

Marvin and Lester started after him. Annie walked to the edge of the porch. "Stop right there and turn around."

"Annie is here after all," Marvin said, grinning at Lester as they turned to face her. His grin evaporated when he saw the rifle aimed at him.

"Annie, what you going to do with that gun?" Lester asked.

"Kill both of you," she said icily.

"Why, Annie girl, you would not hurt us. Your own kin," Marvin said.

"Try me," Annie said sharply.

Lester took a step away from Marvin. "She is bluffing. Let's get her little tail down and take care of her."

"You are two miserable human beings," Bobby said, starting toward them.

"Bobby, stay out of the way. I do not want to shoot you."

Annie sounded like she meant what she said. Bobby wasn't hearing fear in her tone this time. He stepped out of Annie's line of fire.

Annie glared at Marvin and Lester. "You two are rotten excuses for human beings. I am sick and tired of the two of you following me around, threatening me. There's nothing you can do to me anymore. When I get through talking to the sheriff about your visit today, he is going to be looking for both of you again. Get out of the country fast before he comes to take my complaint. Unless you really want to stand there and let me shoot you. I will count to five before I shoot to give you time to get in the buggy. Stay right there if you think I am bluffing. One."

Marvin and Lester shifted from one foot to the other, wanting to call Annie's bluff. She had never acted so defiant toward them before. They couldn't believe she would actually shoot them.

"Two."

Worried now, Lester darted a glance over his shoulder to gage the distance to the buggy.

"Three."

Tom came from behind the house, wondering no doubt about the loud voices. He bristled up and ran at Marvin just as the young man took off running with Lester right behind him. Tom, with his head low, sped after them. He got close enough to fly at Lester's back. Lester howled as Tom stuck his claws through the young man's shirt.

Not looking back, Marvin snapped, "What is wrong with you?"

"A turkey attacked me." Lester shoved Marvin up onto the seat and climbed into the buggy as Annie yelled, "Four."

Marvin yelled at the horse. The buggy lurched forward. He snapped the lines over the horse's back and hurled out of the driveway with Tom in pursuit. Annie screamed, "Five." If the men looked back, she had the rifle aimed at the buggy. In a half second, they were hidden in dust and out of sight.

Tom stopped in the middle of the road, watching and waiting to see if the buggy would turn around and come back. When it didn't, the turkey strutted back into the yard on his way to the hen house.

Annie laid the rifle against the wall and sat down on the porch step. She wiped a hand down her face and tried to regain her composure. Next thing she knew Bobby was in front of her.

"Would you have shot them?" He asked.

"I do not know for sure, but if they came at me or you I might have. I do not want to be beaten up or molested ever again, and I did not want those two bullies to harm you," Annie declared.

"I understand," Bobby said, still puzzled by Annie gathering enough nerve to hold a gun on two human beings.

"Do you? Fighting back is not the Amish way. I was watching back of the living room curtain. You would have let those two beat you up if I had not threatened them," Annie scolded

Bobby ducked his head. "I am not so sure about what I would have done when push came to shove. The bible does say, He who is slow to anger is better than the mighty, and he who rules his spirit is better than he who rules a city."

"That rolls off your tongue so easy Bobby Keim, but I figure God didn't have the Hostellers in mind when he said you should not anger. Those men were going to beat you to a pulp just for the fun of it," she reproached.

"Still if it happened that way I would believe I did the right thing in God's eyes," Bobby countered.

"I doubt you would have been bragging about the fight after all the pain they would have inflicted on you. None of the Hosteller men fight fair, one on one. They always gang up on people. You should know that by now better than anyone else.

Your Amish peaceful way of forgiveness for your enemy might work with other Amish. When you deal with people that have evil hearts like my relatives, you do not stand a chance unless you fight back. This I know," Annie said. "Except I was not strong enough to fight back before when they were ganging up on me. This today was a different matter. I could not let them hurt you."

Bobby eased onto the step beside her and folded his arms on top his knees. "So you were protecting me. I guess should say denki for your help."

Annie reached over with her fingers and touched his bruised

137

jaw. "I guess you are wilkcum."

Bobby said, "The bible says, Be not overcome with evil, but overcome evil with gute."

"I know you believe that, and everything else that is in the bible. Maybe some day I will, too. If it makes you feel any better, I figure I did overcome evil with gute just now, Bobby Keim. I was gute enough to offer Marvin and Lester a chance to leave on the count of five before I shot them."

Bobby grinned at her, and there was a gleaming in his serious eyes that Annie had never seen before. That look made her wonder enough to ask, "What?"

"We have a lot of differences, but you could learn our ways and not just twist them to suit you." His eyes crinkled at the corners as he said wryly, "If you wanted to."

Annie sighed. "That will be a big undertaking, but I have to try if I want to live with the Lapps. They expect me to believe as they do."

Bobby kept watching her. "And what happens later on?"

Annie looked at him curiously. Bobby seemed to driving at something. "I can not tell the future. Can you?"

Bobby looked away. "Nah."

"What were doing over here today anyway?"

"I saw Nurse Hal and Emma go by. I thought John Lapp and the boys might be busy elsewhere. That meant you would be home alone. It seemed like a gute time to come talk to you." He concentrated on the shadows moving across the grass as the breeze shifted the tree branches back and forth. "I have been doing a lot of thinking lately about the future. It had come to the point I think I might bust if I don't talk to you about this." Now he had Annie's attention. "I have been thinking that we know each other pretty gute from all those talks over the fence. Life is different for you now. There comes a time you might want to take a husband so you have a home for you and your baby. I want to take a wife some day soon." His voice quivered as he turned to her. "When you are ready, I would like you to be my sweetheart girl, and I want you to marry me."

138

Annie's mouth flew open. She was pretty sure Bobby had no idea what he'd be getting himself into. "You can not be serious. What man in his right mind would marry me?"

"Me," he said as he took her hand and squeezed it.

"Others say I am second hand goods. I am surprised you asked me and grateful, but I have to think about it." Annie shook her head doubtfully, "I am going to have to prove myself to the Amish community to be accepted. I may never be able to join the church. Is anyone going to forget that I am Joseph Hosteller's daughter since I bear his name? Can they forgive me the violence done to you and the Manwillers, suffered at the hands of my father and the other men? I will be looking over my shoulder for a long time to come for fear some of my family is going to drag me back home like a piece of property taken from them."

"I understand that we need to give you time. I think there will come a day when you are ready to let go of your fears and live life. I will be ready to marry you when that day comes," Bobby said, watching her steadily.

"Still I am second hand goods. If there is anyone who has not heard the stories, all they have to do is see my baby in my arms for proof," Annie argued as she slipped her hand out of his.

"The talk will fade with time. You love your baby and so do I. I will be a gute father to her. My mother and brother will wilkcum you and Beth into our home. I will not bring this up again until you say you are ready to discuss marriage with me. Now I need to go home to help Adam do chores," Bobby said. He started to stand and sat back down. "How gute a shot are you?"

"Fair. Why?"

Bobby had a lilt to his voice when he said, "I just wondered how fast I should run if you decide to shoot at me."

"I would not do that unless I had a gute reason," Annie said flippantly.

Bobby leaned over and kissed her gently on the cheek. "Gute

bye for now."

Annie's mouth dropped open. She felt a hot blush seep into her cheek. She hadn't seen that coming. Bobby didn't look back as he got in his buggy and left. She clamped her hand over that cheek as if to keep the sensation of his lips lingering on her skin.

The girl touched her cheek so many times that evening when she helped Hal do dishes, Hal asked if she had a toothache. Annie blushed. She hadn't realized what she was doing as she thought about Bobby Keim. "Nah, no toothache. Nurse Hal, do you think there is a chance that I can become Amish?"

"I think there is a gute chance now that you're living with us. You will be more comfortable in this community if you learn our ways and be a member of the church," Hal said. "Would you like to talk to Bishop Bontrager about this?"

"Jah."

"I will take you to see him soon," Hal promised.

Chapter 14

A misty film hovered low, blocking out everything from vision past a hundred feet. The fog contained enough moisture to speck up the windshield with a light sprinkle. These days when Hal was out by herself not having a good view of the distance around her made her nervous. Surely Marvin and Lester Hosteller had better sense than to stick around now that Annie had run them off with John's rifle. They had to know the girl meant business. They should be smart enough to leave the country before Sheriff Dawson found them. That was logical to her, but when did the Hosteller men ever seem smart.

It had to be a complete surprise to the Hostellers that the Amish community didn't stand for their home invasions. They didn't expect the Manwillers and Bobby Keim to report them. They didn't see it coming when the law burst in on them and took off the compound leaders. Joseph must have been completely mystified when Annie took the witness stand and testified against him.

Hal knew she'd made it to her destination when she saw the mailbox next to the Mast farm driveway. She had to get her mind back on track. She had an expectant mother to check on. Usually, Eli brought Mary for the monthly visits as they went to Wickenburg to shop. It was time for the third visit. Eli and Mary hadn't stopped by the clinic so Hal wanted to check on Mary.

After examining the new mother to be, Hal said, "One month to go Mary. So far all is well."

Mary lunged herself off the bed. "You will be getting a call from Eli by then for sure. This baby is eager to join the world."

"I can hardly wait to met baby Mast," Hal said, just as excited as Mary was.

"We will make sure you will be the very first one we introduce the baby to," Eli said.

Hal wondered what he meant by that since she would be there when that baby came. She looked at Mary and got a wink. Hal retorted, "Eli, not much chance that I won't be the very first one to see your baby. Even before you and Mary. I'm going to be on the catching end when that baby enters this world. Unless you want to change places with me at the last minute."

Pulling on his small beard as if he was trying to stretch it, Eli replied very seriously, "Do not think I want to change places with you. I give you permission to see the baby first."

"Come to the kitchen. I can fix us ice tea." Mary pushed Eli along in front of her. Hal heard Mary whisper sternly, "Eli, you should not tease Nurse Hal so much."

In the night two weeks later, Hal was awakened by her cell phone rumbling on the dresser top. At first, she thought the noise was a hive of bees until she was fully awake. She didn't want to wake John if she could help it so she eased out of bed and grabbed the phone before she headed to the hall.

She said quietly, "Hello, Nurse Hal."

"This is Eli Mast. Please come right away." Hal heard fear in his voice.

"Mary is bleeding?"

"Nah, she is having cramps."

A baby born now would be all right, but that didn't usually happen. Most first time mothers were two weeks late. Not two weeks early. "Eli, it's a little early to have the baby. Tell Mary to stay in bed. This is probably just premature labor pains. Maybe she had too active a day yesterday. The pains will go away with rest. Don't worry. I'm coming as soon as I can get there."

Hal had to wake John now. He said to tell him where she'd be when she went on a call. She patted his shoulder until he opened his eyes. "I just got an emergency call from Eli Mast. Mary is having pains. I have to go see about her."

She looked at her wrist watch in the glow from the headlight before she got in the car. It was four thirty. She sped to the Mast home. Eli met her at the car with a flashlight. Hal grabbed her nursing bag off the seat. On the way to the house, she asked, "How is Mary now?"

Eli answered, "The pains are harder." When Hal kept going, he grabbed her arm to stop her. "Nurse Hal, you should know Mary can not feel the baby kicking anymore."

Hal found Mary in bed, very still and very pale. At the sight of Hal, her voice trembled. "Please help me. I can not feel the baby moving inside me."

Eli brought the chair in the corner close to the bed for Hal to place the tools of her trade on beside a folded baby blanket. Then he took his place at the head of the bed, holding Mary's hand. Hal pulled her doptone out of her bag. She wanted to see if she could pick up the sound of placental blood rushing in and out of the cord. Louder than that would be the drumming sound of the fetal heart beat. The doptone would magnify the beats, making them easily heard by the mother to relieve her fears. The count of the beats would register on the box screen.

Hal pulled the corded doptone away from the box on the chair and placed it on Mary's stomach. They could hear the swoosh – swoosh as the placental blood flowed, but not the sound of heartbeats. The screen remained blank, not registering the baby's heartbeats. Hal couldn't meet the questioning look in Mary's fearful eyes. She didn't want to be the one to have to say the baby was dead. Not just yet.

143

Not until she'd given herself a lecture anyway. So much for keeping her composure when treating a patient. She'd always been good at doing her job. This time should be no exception. She had to remain strong and professional. She told herself that, but she reminded herself she'd never once thought about what would happen if a baby died when she was in charge of delivery.

Mary was nine centimeters dilated, and the contractions were close together. Delivery would be any time now. She had to tell them before the baby came. The words had to be said out loud so the couple could be prepared. She cleared her throat and looked at the expectant first time parents. She couldn't help the sadness that crept in her voice as she said, "Your baby will be born soon. I don't hear heartbeats, and the doptone screen is blank. The baby isn't living." She didn't have any control over the tears that welled up in her eyes, but she wiped them away the best she could. She had to be able to see what to do next to help Mary.

Eli and Mary looked at each other, the fear had left their faces now that they knew the truth and was replaced by sadness. Eli got on the bed and held Mary as they cried for a few minutes, then they regained their composure and waited for Mary's next contraction.

"How long has it been since you felt the baby move, Mary?" Nurse Hal asked.

"While I was fixing dinner yesterday, the baby was moving and kicking me. When the movements stopped, I just thought the baby was resting. Today, I have not felt movement at all. That is why I worried. Then the pains came."

That meant the death was recent. Chances were the baby might be all right to look at which would help Eli and Mary cope with the death. The bed hadn't been prepared yet. Eli grabbed the folded blue delivery sheet. He helped lift Mary up so they could spread it under her and over the stain made where her water broke earlier.

Hal took Mary's hand. "I must warn you we don't know what

shape the baby is in. Maybe it is deformed. When something is wrong with a baby, it is God's way to let the baby die and deliver early."

"I understand. Whatever the baby looks like, it will be all right," Mary said bravely.

Eli said, "Denki was telling us."

Labor pains hit again and came close together. Mary's face turn red and sweat popped out on her forehead and upper lip. Eli swabbed her face with a cold cloth while Hal watched the other end.

She didn't have time to think about the results while she was busy. This part of delivering a baby was normal. Hal was in sink with the mother, going through the routine coaching ritual. Finally, it was time for the last good push. Nurse Hal's routine to get the mother through the hard painful push was to offer encouragement at the end. "Give me a gute push, Mary, and you can see your ----" She stopped talking, knowing she was only adding to the torture for Eli and Mary.

Mary pushed hard. The baby girl slid out quickly into Hal's hands. Hal worked from instinct when she caught the lifeless baby, laid her on the bed and reached for the suction laying on the chair. She jerked her hand back, knowing suctioning was useless. Still in the routine of a healthy birth, she reached for the folded baby blanket on the chair to warp around the baby to keep her warm. She pulled her hand back again then changed her mind. Life ensuring procedures wouldn't do any good with this baby, but the baby needed a blanket around her so the parents could hold her.

In the mellow glow of the barn lantern, she studied the peaceful, tiny being covered with a silver film. She looked asleep. Such fine features, a tiny bit of blond fuzz on top her head and so much like a fragile porcelain doll. Hal said to the parents, "It's a girl. She has the umbilical cord wrapped around her neck."

A moan from Mary brought on by a cramp came just before the afterbirth expelled. The bloody smell mingled throughout the hot room with acrid sweat from all of them and the fishy smell from when Mary's water broke.

Normally, Amish had family members attending to the mother, and the father stayed right by her side. Hal was used to everything they could think of being done for the mother to make her comfortable during labor. With that last push, all those helpers would grow silent, waiting as they watched for that first deep breath and first cry. Only breathing easy when they saw the baby sucking. That told them the baby was going to be fine.

This baby had just her parents and Nurse Hal with her. Hal stopped attending the mother to study the baby again. No movement. She touched the baby's cool arm. The warmth had gone out of the body just that quick. Her instinct now was to hold the baby close and caress her just as she would any other she delivered, but she didn't know how the parents would want her to act toward their dead baby. She carried the baby to Eli and Mary. She leaned over and showed them the baby's face and where the cord was wrapped around her neck.

They stroked the baby's flannel cover and praise her.

"She looks just like her mother," Eli remarked to Hal.

"What a pretty angel," Mary said softly.

"Look at her tiny ears and sweet face," Eli said.

"I am so sorry she had to struggle to live," Mary said mournfully.

Hal wanted the couple to have some time alone. She told them she wanted to wash the baby and headed to the kitchen. She intended to put baby shampoo on the tiny head and just dip her under the water until she smelled more like a new baby. To her horror when she touched the baby's skin, it started to fall away. When she tried to take the flannel cover away it stuck to the baby's skin, removing a layer. The skin was so fragile, it was melting into the flannel cloth. She didn't have a choice but to stop trying. She took the baby in the flannel cover back to Mary and Eli.

Mary held her arms up. She and Eli were crying again as

they spoke softly to the baby. Finally, Mary came to herself enough to talk with Eli about funeral arrangements. Hal brought in a pan of warm water and washed Mary. She slid the plastic sheet out from Mary and quietly busied herself, packing her nursing bag as she listened.

When Mary's energy was spent, Eli took the baby and sat down on the edge of the bed. He nestled the baby on his knees and rocked slowly back and forth. Mary propped herself up against him to be close. Eli sang to the baby, "Oh, sweet little baby, little baby, oh."

Hal stopped what she was doing. The young couple was grieving, and she grieved, too. She knelt down beside Eli to be apart of the moment and felt tears run down her cheeks again. Eli put his arm around her shoulders. For the longest time, he rocked her, too. The three of them were clueless to the passing of time until at first light, sunshine spilled over the half curtain, and a golden streak fell across the linoleum.

Hal left the Mast house and stepped into the bright sunshine. She didn't want to face the day just yet, but life goes on. She had to stop by Jake and Freda Mullet's farm. She wasn't looking forward to facing Freda with the bad news. When Hal attended quilting bees with Mary's mother, she found the woman a take charge person with an imposing, strong nature that kept her family and those that were around her bending to her will.

Hal understood why Mary was glad that she and Eli had a home of their own to raise their children in. One without Mary's mother looking over the couple's shoulder, bossing them around. In Hal's estimation, Freda's personally was just one step below Stella Strutt's. She knew she didn't have a choice. She had to let the Mullets know what had happened to their grandbaby. Mary would need her mother to help and comfort her.

When she pulled into the Mullet driveway, Freda was on the porch, furiously trying to dislodge the dried mud chore boots had left. She leaned her broom against the porch wall and stood with her hands on her hips as she watched Hal walk toward her. There was a squint to her eyes as she assessed her visitor. Hal figured she noticeably looked like she felt, and that wasn't good.

"Gute morning. Just trying to clean this porch off. Not getting very far with the way the mud dried on. Always a mess on this porch floor. Next rain it will look the same. Come in side and sit down, Nurse Hal," Freda said, holding the screen door open. "Expect John Lapp and the children are doing well. That new baby is fine I know," Freda said, pulling out a chair for Hal at the kitchen table. "You look tired. I will get you a cup of coffee. Expect you want to tell me what brings you here this early and go home to get some rest."

Hal took the way she looked as a clue to Freda that she had been to deliver Mary's baby. Otherwise, Hal didn't have a reason to stop by. Freda was expecting good news.

"I helped deliver Mary and Eli's baby early this morning. The baby was born dead," Hal said.

Freda had picked two cups out of the cupboard and put a hot pad on the handle of the coffee pot. It was as if she just started paying attention to what had been a one sided conversation. She turned to face Hal and folded her arms over her waist. Suddenly, she was really seeing Hal's sad face, and the news soak in. Her face took on a mournful cast as she asked, "Is my daughter all right?"

"Jah."

"What happened?"

Hal studied her hands in her lap. "The cord was around the baby's neck. It died maybe a day before it was born early this morning."

"Are you all right?" Freda looked sincerely concerned.

Hal sighed. "Jah, I think so."

"Well, go home and get some rest. That will help you. I am going to tell Jake to get the buggy hitched up. I need to be with my daughter."

"Jah," Hal agreed as she stood up. "Mary needs you now."

148

Hal found herself back in the car and headed for Wickenburg. She had to fill out a death certificate at the Schrock funeral home then Larry Schrock could go to the Mast farm after the baby.

Mr. Schrock, a middle aged man, met her at the funeral home door. He looked every bit the dignified funeral director in his black suit with a black tie and white shirt. He even sounded like one with his calm, quiet way of speaking that was supposed to comfort the mourners.

Hal introduced herself as an Amish midwife and nurse, and they shook hands. After she filled out the death certificate, she asked as she handed it to Larry Schrock, "Is there anything else I can do for this couple? I haven't had any experience with how the Amish handle a newborn death." His face registered surprise as he studied her Amish clothes. "I wasn't born Amish," Hal said. She added, "I married John Lapp and converted to Amish."

"I was wondering. Let me show you a baby coffin," Larry Schrock suggested as he led her to one of the back rooms. They walked by a row of caskets, all different colors. "Here we are." He pointed to a small coffin. "This is a pine box. We make it as plain as possible with no handles or trimmings and use a gray stain." He opened the lid. "The lining is soft white batiste. We have these made for us strictly to suit the Amish needs."

"Doesn't the Amish make their own clothes and dress the bodies?"

"Yes, for the adults, but we wrap babies in a white downy covering. We can't handle a stillborn very much. Their skins are just too fragile, and we don't want to cause any damage so they can't be dressed," he explained.

Hal said, "I found that out. You may have to leave the flannel coverlet I wrapped her in on the baby. It was stuck to her. I'm sorry, but I didn't know that would happen until it was too late."

Mr. Schrock patted her back. "It's all right. We'll do the best we can for the little one."

149

It was noon by the time Hal got home. She parked the car and walked into the house. Emma came from the kitchen. "Back huh? Dinner is ready whenever you are. I was just going to call Daed and the boys to come."

Hal went to the cradle on the kitchen table and picked up Redbird. The baby started fretting the second she heard her mother's voice. "I'm not hungry right now. Just tired. I think I'm going to sit on the porch and get some fresh air while Redbird nurses."

Emma watched Hal move as if in slow motion. "Hallie, you are not just tired. Something happened at Eli and Mary's. What is it?"

"Mary's baby was dead when it came. The cord was around the baby's neck. I felt so bad for them." Hal heard the strain in her own voice. She couldn't meet Emma's worried eyes.

"Rest now. You can eat when you get ready," Emma said. She followed Hal out to the porch and headed to the barn to let her father and the boys know she had dinner ready.

Hal sat down against the porch post and closed her eyes. As Redbird nursed, she thanked God for her healthy baby. Then she prayed for strength for Eli, Mary and herself to make it through the funeral and in the coming days.

She opened her eyes to find John standing in front of her with his hands jammed in his trouser pockets. Emma herded the boys behind the house to go in the back door so they wouldn't disturb Hal.

John's dark chocolate eyes were filled with concern. "Are you all right, Hal?"

She shook her head slowly no. "I didn't see this day coming, John. I didn't know it would be so hard to have to tell parents their baby is dead before it is born. Eli and Mary were much stronger about the news than I was. Before I started being a midwife why didn't I think about days like this? Maybe I shouldn't be a midwife."

"Can I sit with you?"

"I wish you would. I need a strong shoulder to lean on," she said woefully.

John eased down beside Hal and put his arm around her waist. "You have handled death before many times. It is part of being a nurse."

"That's different from holding a sweet little baby in my hands that I looked forward to bringing into the world and find out it is never going to breathe." She laid her head on his shoulder. "I have to go back to the Mast house tomorrow for the funeral."

"We will all go. You will not be alone," John said quietly. "What happened to the baby? I thought it was doing fine."

"Everything was gute until the baby stopped moving yesterday. The cord wrapped around the baby's neck. By the time Mary started having pains in the night, she thought about not feeling movement. She knew the baby may have died."

John said softly, "Bad enough when it happens. It's worse when you have to watch it happen, ain't? Just know the feeling of grief lessens with time. By the time you deliver another healthy baby, you will again be happy to help bring that baby into the world."

"I don't want to think about going to another delivery right now. I just want to get through tomorrow," said Hal as she choked on a sob.

Hal slept fitfully that night. When morning sent the first gray light through the window, she was up. She quietly went about the morning routine for Redbird and her. There were breakfast and chores to get through, then dressing in their Sunday church meeting clothes and making their way along the dusty country road on that hot August day to the cemetery.

Eli, Mary and their families were already standing by the small pine coffin and open grave. John parked along side the fence. As they walked across the cemetery, they saw several other buggies headed the same way. The procession wasn't very long. Stillborn funerals didn't have as many people show up, mostly just family and a few close friends.

Hal walked toward Eli and Mary, and they came to meet her.

She hugged both of them. While Eli greeted the rest of the family, Mary said, "Nurse Hal, I want you to see our baby now."

Mary lead Hal over by the open grave so she could look down in the coffin. Laying in the downy batiste, the baby was bundled in the white, downy cover from the funeral home. Covering the baby's sparse pale blond hair was the tiny white bonnet. "Mary, she looks so perfect in that little bonnet." Hal patted the cover tenderly. "Precious little one. Rest in peace."

"Eli and I decided to name her Hallie. I hope you do not mind," Mary said shyly.

Hal was surprised. She paused then said, "Nah, I don't mind at all. I am proud to share my name with her."

A woman came up to view the baby with her porcelain white face and blue lips. She said to Mary and Hal, "The little one looks cold. Makes me want to lay another blanket on her."

Mary moved around Hal and hugged the woman. "Denki, for the thought, Sara Zook, but she is not cold in God's hands. My baby is just fine."

Another woman paused long enough to say, "Your baby is an angel in Heaven now."

One woman holding on to her small child's hand came close and lifted the child so she could see the baby.

Finally, the gathering around the grave became quiet. One of the men started the Lord's Prayer, and everyone else joined in. Hal stayed by Mary's side. She found herself wondering what happened to John and that shoulder of his. She needed him to lean on. Hal wrapped her arms around her middle and wished he had stayed closer to her. Suddenly, she felt a strong arm around her shoulders. She opened her eyes, expecting to see John. To her surprise, Eli's father, Butcher Ben Mast, still praying with his head bowed and eyes shut, drew her close to lend her his strength.

Soon the funeral was over. Everyone headed to Eli Mast's house for the dinner.

The next church Sunday at Skinny Dave Yutzy's farm

everyone was visiting in the afternoon. Hal stood at the screen door watching the children play softball when Elton Bontrager singled her out.

"I ate too much dinner," he said when he came up behind her. "Reckon I should go for a walk and maybe walk off some of that gute food."

Hal turned to him. "Are you telling me to move, because I'm blocking the door, Bishop?"

Elton grinned at her. "Nah, I'm inviting you to go for the walk with me."

"I could use some fresh air," Hal said, opening the screen door. As they went down the porch steps, she said, "Where do we want to walk?"

"You pick."

"How about in the orchard. It's shady between those two rows of trees. Maybe there's a cooler breeze in there," Hal said, taking off with Elton beside her.

He walked along slowly with his hands clasped behind his back. "How are you?"

"All right, Bishop Bontrager."

"You do not look it," Elton said bluntly. "The bubbling joy is gone from your spirit and your step."

"Perhaps you could say that about most of the people here. We've had a lot to deal with lately, worrying about the Hostellers."

"That is so. Right now I am thinking about a deeper sadness when someone loses their baby. I visited the Mast couple after the funeral. Such a caring young couple. Would you believe their concern was more for you than themselves?"

"Me? I'm sorry if they have been worried about me," Hal said sincerely. "Elton, forever more I'll be wondering with every birthing if I'm going to have to go through helping a couple only to tell them the baby died."

"I understand that. If you did not feel so deeply about what you do when you are helping others there would be something wrong with you. Your deep caring is what makes you a gute nurse. No doubt this sad event will happen again though I can say, if it helps you, I have not had so many funerals for stillborns as you might think. When this happens to you remember to think God willed it to be so. The death was not your fault, or was there anything you could do to prevent it. Life goes on, and the Masts will have other babies. This is our way of dealing with the loss of a baby."

"That is what I said to the Mast couple," Hal told him.

"Gute. That is when they told me their concern was for you. Want to know what I told them?"

Hal stopped and faced him. "Sure."

"I said not to worry about Nurse Hal. She will bounce back. It is just part of her nature. When the next mother calls her for help, Hal will grab that odd color of green nursing bag that has written on it 'Life Is A Blast' and go."

Watching the robins flit over through the fruit trees, Hal gave that some thought. She grinned. "You're right, Elton. So stop worrying. I'm going to be fine. So my nursing bag is an odd color of green, huh?"

Elton laughed. "I figured that might strike a cord with you."

Chapter 15

One summer afternoon, Annie laid the mop up against the house and called to Hal hoeing in the garden. "Nurse Hal, are you about done?"

"Jah."

"I wondered when we could go talk to the bishop about me becoming Amish," Annie said.

"I'm sorry. With all that's been going on I forgot about that. Let's clean up and go," Hal said, propping her hoe next to the mop. "Emma can watch the babies while we're gone."

About a half hour later, Hal had harnessed Ben and hooked him to the buggy. She pulled in front of the house. Annie climbed in and had just pulled the door shut when they heard a loud thud.

"What was that?" Hal asked.

"Something hit my door." Annie peered out her window. "Oh."

"Oh what?"

"I guess Tom did not want us to leave home. He is beside the buggy, all bristled up," Annie said, scrunching up her face.

"We aren't going to ask him to go with us. That's for sure," said Hal. She clicked to Ben.

As they drove to the end of the driveway, Annie watched from her window. "Tom is chasing us. He looks mad."

Hal turned the buggy onto the road. At the back end of the buggy, they heard a loud clunk. Hal looked puzzled. "Now what?"

"That was Tom again. He flew up and attacked the buggy," Annie declared.

"I sure hope he's in a better mood when we go home," Hal said dryly.

"Me, too, Nurse Hal. We might have to stay in the buggy until Daniel makes Tom go to the chicken house," Annie said, grinning.

"Annie, there is something I've wanted to bring up. Now that you are a member of the Lapp family, Emma and you are getting close just like sisters. I know the boys think of you as a sister. Redbird and Beth will grow up as sisters. I think of you as my daughter. Do you think you could call me something besides Nurse Hal? Emma calls me Hallie. The boys call me Mama Hal and John calls me Hal. Take your pick or choose another name."

Annie thought for a moment. "I've never really had a mother before. Not one like you. I'd like to call you Mama Hal."

"I'd be proud to have you do that," Hal said. "I know John would like to be called Papa John."

"Are you excited about changing to Amish?" Hal asked.

"More like nervous and anxious. We both know that I am not the best person in the mind of this community," Annie said.

"Now don't run yourself down. It will surprise you how many Plain people have respect for you. They see the way you are living your life now. Not only that they are grateful to you for testifying against your relatives so everyone feels safe again. You helped put the Hostellers in prison so they wouldn't harm anyone else. I think the bishop sees it that way, too," Hal assured her.

"I hope so. There is more to my wanting to become Plain than that I live with you now," Annie said.

"Oh?" Hal said, looking straight ahead. She hoped she knew what Annie was leading up to.

"Remember the day that Bobby Keim came over and ran into Marvin and Lester coming out of the house."

"Jah, I remember. Come to think about it I've wondered what he came for that day. I never heard," Hal said.

"Bobby thought I would be home alone. He wanted to talk to me. Nurse ----. Sorry, Mama Hal, he wants to marry me," Annie said quietly.

"Really!" Hal exclaimed, smiling. Then she saw how sober Annie looked. "Oh, what did you tell him?"

"I told him first I had to work on being a better person. One with more strength. Besides, I am second hand goods now. His choice of brides might not be accepted by the church community," Annie said honestly.

"What did Bobby say?" Rushed out of Hal's mouth.

"He said he thought I was worrying for nothing, but he would wait until I was ready to say I would marry him," Annie said.

"Bless that young man. He is so kind and understanding. If you let him get away Annie Hosteller you will be sorry," Hal admonished. "Don't wait too long to tell him jah. Oh, if that is what you want of course."

Annie grinned at her. "Jah, Bobby Keim is what I want."

Under her breath, Hal muttered, "Yeah!"

They drove into the Bontrager yard. The thud of an ax whacked wood behind the house. Jane met Annie and Hal at the door. "Nice afternoon for a visit."

"It is that," Hal agreed. "We've come to talk to the bishop. Is he around?"

"Out back chopping wood. He has been at it for a gute long while. About time he came in for a rest." Jane stuck her head out the back door. "Elton, Hal and Annie are here to see you. Come in and get a glass of ice tea."

Jane had time to serve Hal and Annie before Elton came in, wiping sweat from his flushed face on a blue handkerchief.

"You came to visit just in time. I needed a break," he said, smiling at them.

"Seems to me, Elton, someone told you to take it easier now that you've had a heart attack," Hal admonished.

"So you did, Nurse Hal. Sometimes I forget," Elton said sheepishly. "Now what can I do for you?"

"Annie would like to become a member of the Plain church now that she is part of the Lapp family. We wanted to know if that would be possible," Hal explained.

Elton Bontrager brushed his hand down his beard while he hesitated. "I have to bring this matter up before a member meeting after church. If the members vote agreeably, Annie can take the classes and be baptized into the church." He looked at Annie, "This is what you want, ain't?

"Jah, I want it," Annie said shyly.

"How are you doing since most of your family went to jail for a long time? Does it make it easier for you?"

"I am feeling much better. Mama Hal and the rest of her family are so very gute to me. I feel at last I have a family who cares about me," Annie said.

Elton told her, "Whenever we are troubled and life has lost its song it's God testing us with burdens just to make our spirit strong."

Her voice trembled. "My spirit is stronger than it was, but I fear all that moves around me and every shadow, thinking some of the men are going to attack me. Night is the worst time. I wake up listening for footsteps in the hall that might be one of the men coming into my room. That feeling is so hard to get shut of."

"Terrible thing is fear. It gnaws away at your strength until there is nothing left to live for if you let it. You have to be strong enough to not let that happen," the bishop said.

"For so long my father and brothers thought they had the right to do whatever they wanted to all of us. I do not feel as if the fear will ever leave me. I hate all of them for what they did to us," Annie said, her voice filled with anguish.

"Annie, you are a gute girl. You must learn not to hate if you want to be a Plain church member. Not hating those men is the first step toward learning to be a forgiving person. It is our way to forgive all that anyone does to us. Give it time."

"Denki, Bishop. I will try to be a better person," Annie said sincerely.

The next Sunday church meeting, Bishop Bontrager's message was about weighing the worth of people individually. He quoted from the bible, "As his name is so is he. That is from the book of Samuel."

We know people by the name of Hosteller that have tried their brand of terror on us and failed. Some of those among you may say we broke the Ordnung laws by going to the authorities. I say to you we did not break our laws. The Hosteller men were not of our faith. They would not have stopped their bullying ways if we peacefully prayed for them and forgave them for what they did. We had no choice but to talk to the sheriff.

The bible says, "Let justice roll down like water's righteousness, like a mighty stream on those men who harm you." That is what happened. Englischer law took the matter out of our hands and arrested the Hostellers. They have been tried in court and sent to prison for all their crimes.

In Proverbs the bible says, When justice is done, it is a joy to the righteous but dismay to evildoers. And so I believe at this time it is so for the Hosteller men as they look from behind jail bars. Now church is adjourned.

There will be a member meeting now. All that are not members are dismissed. This meeting is to decided if Annie Hosteller can become a member of our church.

As soon as the children left the room, Bishop Bontrager began again. "I repeat from the book of Samuel again, 'As is her name so is Annie Hosteller'. She bears the Hosteller name, but she was a victim. She should not have to pay the price of shunning by Plain people, or Englischers because of what happened to her as a defenseless child just because her name is

159

Hosteller.

The Lapp family has taken Annie and her baby in as their own and given them a home. Annie and the Lapps would like her and her baby to be a part of their faith, the Plain people's church. The Lapps are giving Annie guidance and love in order to live on the right path. She needs a faith to sustain her along that path. This church can give her that. Tell me how do you vote?"

For the most part, the members were understanding and sympathetic. They voted to let Annie be a member of the church. After all, the Lapp family opinion of the girl went a long ways with them. They respected John and Hallie Lapp for taking in that homeless girl and her baby.

Stella Strutt said Annie committed adultery and there was not any way of getting around that. She had a child out of wedlock to prove it. Those things are against the Ordnung. She voted nay.

Bobby Keim had voted with the men before Stella got a say. He voted yes. He made it clear that Annie was a victim and in no way responsible for what happened to her. She deserved a better life as part of the Lapp family and their church community. That balanced out the nay vote from Stella.

When the votes were all taken, the vote came out in Annie's favor. The time for Annie's lessons would be set by the bishop. She was allowed to join in on any social gathering she chose like other young people waiting to be baptized.

It was good to hear Annie actually humming in the kitchen just like Emma. What a difference a few months had made in that girl's personality. Annie truly was one of the family now that she felt as if she belonged. Annie's life was so much better she had stopped having nightmares.

Hal couldn't remember what life was like without the girl. She was so glad that Annie and Beth were part of their family. Of course, she was going to just get used to having Annie help her instead of Emma, and the girl would marry and move out.

That would be all right, too, once Hal quit missing her and

the baby being under their roof. She'd still have a daughter and a grandchild along with a new son-in-law. They would be over to visit often. Hal just knew it. The important thing was Annie was going to have a good life. The past was behind her. Annie's future was going to be perfect.

One Sunday morning at breakfast, John must have thought about getting several uninterrupted nights of sleep. "Annie, did you sleep gute last night?"

"Jah, I did, Papa John," she answered.

"You will sleep even better from now on with so much work to do," he said. "Nothing like a hard day's work to make you tired enough to rest."

"Jah, you are right," Annie replied.

That afternoon, the Lapp family came home after church at the Daniel Miller farm. Emma offered to pop corn to snack on before chores and asked Annie to help her.

Emma picked up an arm load of wood from the box behind the cookstove to build the fire while Annie went for the skillet. She slapped one last stick on top the arm load and felt a sharp stab in her eye. She dropped the wood back in the box. "Ouch!"

"What happened?" Annie asked.

Emma was holding her hand over her left eye. "I just got a sliver of wood in my eye. It sure smarts. Can you build the fire? I am going to wash my eye out."

Annie hustled to start the fire and find a lid so she could pop the corn. Emma splashed water in her eye and dried her face.

"Is your eye better?" Annie asked.

Emma squinted at her. "Not much, but the wood scratched my eyeball I guess." She took over shaking the hot skillet. When the popping stopped, she poured the popcorn in a dishpan. "Annie, you are in charge of seasoning. Shake on plenty of salt and be generous with the butter."

As soon as supper was over, Annie and Emma had planned to take Bobby and Adam Keim to the buddy group singing that Daniel Miller's children were hosting.

When the time come to leave, Emma had been holding her hand over her left eye for awhile. Hal asked, "Emma, just how bad does that eye hurt you?"

"Some," Emma said,

"Let me look," Hal ordered. Emma took her hand away. Her eye was red and swollen shut. "Some might be an understatement. You didn't get that sliver out of there. I'm going to wash your eye out again."

"All right. Annie, you might as well go on without me. I really do not feel like going," Emma said regretfully.

"I hate to go without you," Annie told her.

"If you aren't comfortable going out alone, you shouldn't," Hal said.

"I just wish Emma could come is all. I will be fine by myself, besides once I get to the Keim farm Bobby and Amos will be with me," Annie said.

"I can take Beth to my room at bedtime," Emma offered. "That is where she will be when you get home."

Annie felt nervous as she drove the buggy by the Hosteller farm but all seemed quiet. Not too many people lived there anymore. Most of them had left after the Hostellers went to jail. The rest hoped they would be left to live in peace. She knew she had to suspress her fears. She had a pleasant evening ahead of her.

Bobby and Adam Keim were waiting on the porch steps for her to come. They were eager to get to the sing along. The boys had to know why Emma wasn't along and felt bad about her eye hurting her.

The evening went well. Annie enjoyed herself and Bobby stayed right with her. They sat across from each other at the dating table. Adam sat at the singles table. He couldn't sing, but he smiled and clapped his hands to the songs.

Annie parked in front of the Keim house about nine thirty that night. Bobby got out of the front seat with Annie and Adam slipped from the back.

Annie said, "Bobby, could I talk to you for a minute?"

"Jah, more than a minute if you want. Go on in, Adam. I'll be there soon," he said as he climbed back in the buggy.

Annie clamped her lips together and stared out the windshield.

"Annie, your minute is about up, and I can not read your mind," Bobby said.

"This is a big step for me," she said nervously.

Bobby was worried. "You have made many big steps lately and each has made you a different and better person. What is this step?"

Annie scooted herself around on the seat until their knees touched. She wanted to watch his face while she talked. "You said you would not push me to marry you until I was ready. I needed time to come to grips with my past life. After that, I had to take the classes and be baptized in the church. I have made it through that, and now I find myself accepted by people like at the singing tonight. Oh, I had such a good time."

Bobby frowned as he said, "I am glad. Are you trying to tell me you will never marry me now that you have a chance to find another man?"

The tone of his voice and words surprised Annie. "Nah, silly. I'm trying to tell you I am ready to marry you if you still want me."

In a small voice, Bobby said, "Oh, you scared me. Do you always need to take the long way around to a direct question? Of course I want to marry you. I love you."

"I am glad to here it," Annie said, giggling. "I love you, too."

"Now see if you can answer this question with the shortest answer possible so I do not fall over in a fit of apoplexy. Will you marry me, Annie Hosteller?"

Annie hesitated long enough for Bobby to narrow his eyes at her, filled with impatience. She said, "Jah."

"Jah, what?"

Her voice filled with humor. She said, "I could have said more, but a one word answer was what you said wanted. Jah, I

163

will marry you, Bobby Keim."

Bobby put his hand behind Annie's neck and drew her close. He kissed her. "That was one of many kisses for many years to come, Annie. Now I should go in before my mother notices I am still out here alone with you. Are you going to be all right going home? I would go with you if you want."

Annie lifted her chin high. "The old days of me being a frightened mouse are over. I have no reason to hide on this lovely night. Go in and sleep well, Bobby Keim."

The buggy was warm so she left the door open to get the slight bit of night air as she circled Ben around in the driveway. She sang a song as she drove past the Hosteller farm. Maybe not so much to bolster her courage, but in defiance even though there was not a soul close enough to hear her.

It was such a special summer night. The stars winked in good humor at her from the black sky as if thrilled with Bobby and her upcoming marriage. The full moon bathed the road in a yellow glow about as strong as the headlights did. Millions of lightning bugs sparkled around her, adding magic to the night. Annie, for the first time, knew real joy and love instead of fear. All was right in her world. Bobby Keim loved her, and soon they would announce their wedding date in church. She was getting married. She'd have a good husband, and Beth was going to have a loving father.

Before she knew it the intersection was coming up. Annie slowed down to turn toward home. As she made the bend, an impact of something smacked the side of her head hard, entered her skull and exploded inside. She screamed and fell sideways onto the seat. Her scream frightened Ben. The horse picked up speed. Annie thought that was good. She needed to get home fast. She reached up to touch the side of her head and felt a warm sticky substance running down her face.

It took all the energy she had to upright herself. She'd lost the lines, but that didn't matter now. Whatever was wrong she knew she had to get to Nurse Hal fast. Her vision was fuzzy, and her head was one big splitting pain. She felt faint so she leaned back and sideways so her head was outside the buggy to let the breeze wash over her.

She realized when Ben slowed down and then stopped. She opened her eyes and looked around. The house was dark. Everyone was in bed. She had to try to walk to the house and get help. She slid off the seat and felt the jar as her feet by passed the step. She hit the ground with a painful thud She took a step or two, went to her knees and collapsed. She tried to will herself to get back up, but she couldn't make herself move. She wanted to cry for help, but she couldn't make her voice work anymore.

The thought came to her that the Lapp family would be looking for her soon. They would take care of her when they found her. That made her feel safe and calm. Faint stars cavorted into a dazzling display of circling lights just before everything in Annie's world turned to darkness. In a few seconds, Annie lost consciousness.

Chapter 16

John's alarm clock went off. Hal rubbed her eyes and groaned. "That sure seemed like a short night."

"They all do lately," John said as he grinned at her. "Reckon that comes with age."

"Did you hear Annie come home last night?" Hal asked, stepping into her slip.

"Nah," he said.

Hal finished dressing and went to wake the others. She opened Annie's bedroom door. "Annie, time to get up." When she didn't get a reply, she walked over to the bed. Annie wasn't there. The bed hadn't been slept in. She rushed back to their room. "John, Annie didn't come home last night. Something happened to her."

"Now do not panic until we find out what happened," John said. "Maybe she crawled into bed with Emma."

"Jah, I'll see." Hal stepped into Emma's room and asked, "Emma, you awake?"

"Jah."

"Annie is not in here. I hoped she was in bed with you," Hal said in a strained voice. "She did not sleep in her bed last night."

166

"The baby slept all night so I am just now waking up. Wonder what happened to Annie?"

"We have to look for her," Hal said on her way to the boys room. "Noah and Daniel, get up. We have to find Annie. She's not home yet."

The boys feet bounced onto the floor. By the time Hal had the cradle down the stairs, John was putting his shoes on and Noah was headed for the porch door with Daniel behind him.

The boys froze in the open door. Naoh exclaimed, "Daed, the buggy is here. Ben is pulling it around in a circle. Daniel, come help me stop the horse."

They raced across the yard. The buggy rolled away from them. That's when they saw Annie. Her head was in a pool of blood. They raced back to the house, screaming for Mama Hal.

John and Hal knelt beside Annie. John cried, "What could have happened to her?"

Emma rushed to them and handed Hal her nursing bag. Swiftly, Hal checked for pulse in the girl's neck. "Annie has a head wound to the side of her head. Maybe she fell out of the buggy and hit her head if Ben started up too quick before her feet were on the ground. She's still alive." Hal rummaged in her bag for her cell phone and called the ambulance. Then she bandaged Annie's head to try to stop the flow of blood.

It seemed forever before the ambulance screamed in and back toward the hospital. Hal said, "I want to take the car. It's much faster than the buggy. Besides, Ben looks like he's worn out."

"Emma and me will go with you. Noah and Daniel, stay here and do the milking," John told them.

"Is that all we have to do?" Noah asked.

"You can pray," John said, gravely serious.

The ambulance had unloaded Annie before the Lapp family got to the hospital. The ER doctor, Stan Christensen came to meet them in the waiting room. "Annie's been taken for a scan on her head. We may have to operate so I've called a neurosurgeon from Des Moines. By the time he arrives, we should have Annie stable. She needs a few units of blood. I'll be back when I know more."

An hour later, Dr. Christensen walked in briskly. "The scan showed she has a bullet in her brain. I can't give you much hope she will live after we operate or that she will make it through surgery."

"Do what you can," John told him. After the doctor left, John tried to digest what happened. "Someone shot her. Why?"

"I knew it wasn't a good idea for Annie to be out alone on that road. I felt it last night. Why didn't I make her stay home," Hal said. "It must have been Marvin Hosteller that shot her. He hasn't been caught yet."

Emma said, "If only I had been with her this might not have happened."

"Might be both of you would have been shot," John said. "If it was Marvin, he would not be choosy how many he harmed."

A few hours later, Sheriff Dawson came to the waiting room. "Hi, folks. I got a call from Doc. Christensen that a shooting victim had been brought in by the name of Annie Hosteller."

John said, "We found her laying in the driveway this morning. She went to a singing last night. We do not know when she came home."

"How do you think this happened?" The sheriff asked.

"We wondered where Marvin Hosteller is right now. We are afraid it is him did this out of revenge," John said.

"I'm going out to the Hosteller farm and look around. I'll have a talk with neighbors out that way," the sheriff told him.

"Would you stop by Bishop Bontrager's place and tell him about Annie. He might be able to help. Go by the Keim farm and tell Bobby. He and Annie were gute friends," Hal said.

"Yes, ma'am. How's Annie doing?"

"She is in surgery to remove the bullet. Most of her blood is in our driveway. The doctor doesn't give us much hope," Hal told him.

"I'm sorry to hear that. So when did you find Annie?"

"Early this morning. The horse had been pulling the buggy

in a circle around Annie for hours," John said.

"I'll get back to you folks when I find out anything. You can count on it," Sheriff Dawson told them.

Later that afternoon, the doctor was back. He said, "We got the bullet out. Annie is still alive, but her brain is swelling. I have to tell you the prognosis is not good. We don't think we can save her. She is in ICU on life support now. She may never regain consciousness. You can sit with her if you want. The nurse will take you to the room.

Mr. Lapp, the bullet has been taken to the sheriff department. If the weapon is found, the ballistic match will help prove who shot the gun."

They filed into the ICU room and walked softly to the bed. Annie's head was covered with a turban of bandages. Her pale face listed to the side. When Hal picked one limp hand up and Emma the other, there wasn't any warmth in them. Hal and Emma bowed her head and said a silent prayer for Annie.

Sheriff Dawson and his deputy, Roy Iverson, drove to the Lapp farm to start his investigation. Noah and Daniel trotted from the house to meet them.

"Howdy, fellows. Remember me? I'm Sheriff Dawson," the sheriff said. "We are here about Annie. Deputy Iverson and I are going to have a look around."

Noah asked somberly, "Do you know how Annie is? Daed and Mama Hal have not come back from the hospital yet."

Sheriff Dawson took his hat off and swiped a hand over his head. "Your folks might be at the hospital for a spell. Annie is not doing too good." He hated to be the one to tell them, but the boys needed to know the truth. He hated speaking even worse when he saw tears in their eyes. "Listen, you two might be able to help me with this investigation to find out who shot Annie. Want to do that?"

"Jah," Noah said hoarsely.

"All right then. Who found Annie?"

Noah said, "I did. Daniel and me looked out the door. The

horse was pulling our buggy around in a circle. I ran out to catch him and saw Annie laying in the road."

"Show us where," the sheriff said. The boys lead the way a few feet from where they stood. Sheriff Dawson squatted down and looked at the puddle of blood. "Appears Annie was in that spot for a good long while."

Daniel nodded. "She went to a singing last night. She should have been home by bedtime."

"Your family didn't notice when she didn't come home?" Roy Iverson asked.

Noah nodded. "We all went to bed. We thought Annie would come in soon."

Deputy Iverson looked at the driveway. "The buggy wheels had time to do a lot of circling from the looks of all the grooves in the tracks."

"I see that," the sheriff said. He noticed drips of blood along the driveway. "Can we see the buggy, boys?"

Noah said, "It is parked in the lean-to off the north end of the barn. We can show you."

The lawmen looked the buggy over. The seat was covered with blood and splatters were on the windshield. "It's clear Annie was shot while in the buggy," the sheriff said. "Noah, do you remember if the door was open or shut this morning."

Noah hesitated a moment. "The door was open."

"So Annie must have left the door open on the way home and then collapsed in the driveway on her way to the house," the sheriff said. "Now Roy, how about we follow those blood drops in the driveway just to see how far they go."

"Can we go with you?" Noah asked.

The sheriff wrinkled his nose at that, but as he studied the forlorn boys, he gave in. "Yes, but stay behind Roy and me. I don't want you to step in some evidence."

The men walked slowly west down the road with Noah and Daniel behind them. The sheriff pointed out a splatter of blood each time he saw one. They soon came to the Bontrager farm.

"Roy, you want to stop in and tell Bishop Bontrager what's

going on. John Lapp wanted him to know. I'll keep going. If we have too much traffic down this road, that would cover up the blood. Catch up with us when you're done here."

Not too far on, they came to the intersection. "Stop where you are boys until I tell you." Sheriff Dawson turned in a circle. He walked from the intersection south for a few yards then back tracked. He pointed down to a large blood spot in the middle of the intersection by buggy tracks. "Here was where Annie was shot. Right as she was making the turn toward home. The blood spots started here. We can go back by Bontragers and get Roy on our way to your place."

Roy Iverson met them at the end of the driveway. "Elton Bontrager told me he heard a gun shot last night about ten. He remembered the time because it was when he was getting ready for bed. He said the shot sounded some distance away and came from the west."

The sheriff nodded. "That sounds right. The blood spots begin in the next intersection as Annie went to turn. That bullet went in the buggy and hit her in the head."

The lawmen drove over to Bobby Keim's house and gave him the bad news. They explained what they found so far and asked him to tell John Lapp at the hospital. That way they wouldn't have to bother the family right now.

Bewildered and out of his element, John twisted his straw hat in his hands and helplessly surveyed all the life support hooked to Annie. So many different noises; hums, clicks and whirs. Soft though the guardians of Annie's fragile life were, they blended to block out the room's silence.

The door opened, and a nurse escorted Bobby Keim in. Emma rushed to take his hand. "Bobby, the doctor does not think Annie will live." He grimaced, thinking what she said couldn't be so. Emma led him over to the bed. He stared down at Annie in disbelief. Emma laid his hand she held over on Annie's and tears streamed down Bobby's face. Just looking at Annie, Bobby knew Emma's words most likely were true unless God willed that Annie should live.

Bobby turned his attention to John and Hal. "I was coming to see you soon to tell you Annie and me would like to marry. She told me last night she was ready for the wedding. I have never seen her so happy. Her face glowed in the moonlight. Now how could this be?" He asked in anguish.

"We don't have the answers to that, Bobby," Hal told him. "I was always taught that hearing remains intact no matter how ill a person becomes. I think we should leave you alone with Annie for awhile. You talk to her. Knowing you're here will be the comfort she needs right now. Come, John and Emma."

They were in the waiting room when Bishop Bontrager and Jane came. The nurse pointed to where the Lapp family waited. After comforting the family, the Bontragers asked to see Annie so the Lapps took them to the ICU room. The bishop shook hands with Bobby Keim and picked up Annie's hand. Jane took the other one. They stayed by her side while the bishop said a prayer for Annie, then they said they'd go home and wait to hear from John.

Through the night, Bobby held Annie's hand as he prayed for a miracle. While the others sat in seats along the ICU room wall. With the start of the new day, Doctor Christensen came in. He examined Annie before he turned to the row of sleepy people, waiting expectantly. "I hate to tell you this folks, but Annie is brain dead. The only way her heart and lungs will continue to work is by keeping her on life support. She is never going to wake up again, and this is not the quality of life a young woman would want."

John said, "What is it we should do?"

"If I were her family, I'd take her off life support and let her pass away peacefully."

John turned to Hal. "What do you say?"

"Doc is right. We should let Annie go for her sake not ours," Hal said. "Bobby, what do you think?"

"My heart says nah, but my head says jah. My Annie will be better off with God now," Bobby said, his voice filled with a deep sorrow.

"Jah, that is right," Emma told him as she rubbed his back.

"All right, we will turn off all the machines. Annie will live for maybe a few hours until her heart stops naturally," Dr. Christensen told them.

"We will stay and pray for her until Annie dies," John said.

Hal suggested that Noah and Daniel would like to be there to tell Annie good bye. She told John she would after the boys and be right back.

Noah and Daniel had just finished milking when Hal drove in. The boys ran from the barn to meet her. She put her arms around them as she explained Annie was not going to live long. She told them to hurry and change into clean clothes so they could go to the hospital with her to say good bye.

Without the noisy machines, Annie's raspy breathing was very noticeable. About three in the afternoon, the girl stopped breathing. The quiet in the room was as noticeable as the stillness of a gentle snowfall.

Her adopted family and Bobby Keim made a circle around her bed. Hal held Annie's hand with John by her side. Noah took John and Daniel's hand. Daniel reached across the foot of the bed to take Emma's hand. She held Bobby's and he held Annie's hand. With the circle completed, they recited the Lord's Prayer.

Then the group made that long walk down the hall to the nurse's station. Lucy Stineford took funeral arrangement information. She'd call the funeral home and Schrock's Funeral director would be there soon for Annie.

The next morning, Mr. Schrock was out to the Lapp farm early in his horse drawn hearse, carrying Annie in a pine coffin. Elton Bontrager, Luke and Levi Yoder helped Mr. Schrock place the coffin on boards laid on two chairs. The visitation and funeral were to be in the living room.

Jane Bontrager, Linda and Margaret Yoder waited for the men to leave so they could dress Annie. They put on Annie the white dress and apron that Emma had worked on all night and the new prayer cap Annie had sewed for herself. The evidence that showed Annie horrible demise, the hideous wound in the side of her head, couldn't be hidden by the prayer cap and the funeral director's makeup.

When news about Annie passed around, Plain people were afraid to venture from home alone again, fearing Marvin Hosteller had committed the horrible crime. The buggies showed up as one big procession to honor this brave young woman that had been through so much and with God's help over came it all until he called her to Heaven.

During the funeral service, John and Hal made sure the Keim family sat with their family around the coffin. Word was passed that Bobby Keim was Annie's intended sweetheart.

After the trip to the cemetery, everyone came back to the Lapp home for the dinner. Dishes of food, loaves of bread, pies and cakes filled the table and the counters.

While the women readied the meal and served the men then the children, they visited as if it were a church meeting Sunday. Jane Bontrager praised the bountiful crop of apples that the women had turned into apple butter at her house. Edna Mast said the women's help at the quilting folic made it easy for her to finish the quilt they had worked on. Jonah Stolfus's wife, Freda, told them they should be pleased with their hard work when they came to her house to can their tomato crop. Everyone left with enough jars of juice and tomatoes to last them all winter.

While the women ate dinner, Hal was quiet. The women understood, she was in mourning.

Margaret said to no one in particular, "Such a sad thing we have faced to say good bye to this girl that we have all come to respect and like."

"Jah," Jane Bontrager agreed. "Sometimes, it is hard to understand God's plan."

Hal stopped scooting the food around on her plate. "We all will miss Annie. A big hole has been left in my family. Annie's life was going so well. We were so looking forward to a wedding. Annie was happy that Bobby Keim asked her to marry him. They were going to announce the wedding soon." Hal sighed. "It just doesn't seem fair that Annie isn't here to enjoy her life after all she went through."

Jane patted Hal's hand. "God holds the plan for all of us. This was his plan for Annie. He needed her in Heaven."

Shy Mary Mast spoke up. "You have been left with a part of Annie to treasure. You still have her baby."

Hal saw the sadness on the young woman's face and knew Mary was thinking about her own empty arms.

"You are right, Mary. We will treasure baby Beth and raise her so that her mother would be proud of her," Hal said.

The men talked in low somber tones about what they must try to do to keep this horrible accident from happening to them.

Hamish Manwiller rubbed his evenly trimmed but much shorter beard. "Can what happened to Annie be Marvin Hosteller's doing out of revenge?"

"We have no way of knowing until the sheriff finishes his investigation," John said.

"If it is Marvin Hosteller, he will not stop until he has others in his rifle sights," Butcher Ben Mast predicted.

Hamish's complexion paled. "My wife and me top the list, I fear, along with Bobby Keim and Nurse Hal for testifying at the trial."

Elton Bontrager said, "Until we know what happened for sure, we must be careful. Do not travel anywhere you can put off. I remember hearing a gun shot Friday night and didn't know the tragedy that shot had caused."

"You heard the shot that killed our Annie?" John gasped.

"Jah, Jane and me were getting ready for bed. Had to be close to ten that night. Best I could tell the shot was fired west of our house, but quite aways off. I wondered who would be firing a gun that time of night. I wished I had known about Annie."

Chicken Plucker Jonah Stolfus listened intently. "This was a

175

sad thing," he said to no one in particular.

"Nothing any of us can do now," John said sorrowfully. "We all slept through the night in our beds upstairs not knowing Annie was suffering right outside our door. The doctor assured us, with as bad as her brain was damaged, even if we had found her right away that much time would not have helped."

Chicken Plucker Jonah listened with his head bowed. Finally, he said, "I am so sorry for your family's loss, John."

"Life goes on," the bishop said. "We will go on, too. That is our way."

A week later, Sheriff Dawson's patrol car parked at the Lapp farm. The tall man unfolded from the front seat and looked around. John came from the hog pen to meet him. Hal watched from the kitchen window with Emma. They knew this had to be about Annie.

John pointed toward the house, and they walked to the door. Hal rushed to let them in. "Sheriff Dawson, I suppose you have news for us about Annie's shooter."

Emma asked, "Did you catch Marvin Hosteller?"

The sheriff took his hat off and gripped it in his hands. "It wasn't Marvin Hosteller that shot Annie, and we haven't caught him yet," he answered Emma.

"Sheriff Dawson, who would do such a thing to our Annie?" Hal cried.

"That's what I came to tell you folks, ma'am. This was just a freak accident. A farmer, Jonah Stolfus and his wife came to my office last week. Maybe you know them."

"Jah, we do. Jonah and Freda belong to our church community. Their farm is a couple miles west of here," John said, puzzled by where the sheriff was going with this.

The sheriff nodded agreement. "Best we can figure, the Stolfus farm is a mile and a half away from that intersection up the road from you. Mr. Stolfus thought he might have shot Annie. He came to turn himself in."

"From that far away to hit Annie. How could that be? Ah, nah. Even so, Jonah would not harm anyone. He couldn't do that. That can not be so," John declared.

"Sheriff," Hal said. "We know Jonah would not do such a thing."

"You're right, ma'am. He wouldn't if he had been aware of what would happen. This was one of those weird accidents. Jonah says he fired his muzzle loader in the air after he cleaned it that night to see if it was working properly. He was getting the gun ready for deer season. He'd thought for awhile about what happened to Annie. When Elton Bontrager talked about the time he heard the shot at Annie's funeral, Jonah wondered if his shot hit her. He came in willingly and gave us his gun for testing. The muzzle loader's shot matched the lead ball that was in Annie's head. Jonah and his wife are very upset. He had no idea that ball would travel so far. I hope you understand I didn't press charges against Mr. Stolfus. I believe this was just an accident."

John declared, "I do understand. We know that Jonah did not mean to harm our Annie."

"Poor Jonah and Freda. They must be beside themselves," Hal said sympathetically.

"Sheriff, my family will go this day and tell them we understand," John said.

"That's good." The sheriff paused. "I've been wondering. What's going to become of Annie Hosteller's baby?"

"We are going to raise her as our own," John said. "That is what Annie would have wanted."

"She has become as much a part of our family as Annie was," Hal told him.

"That is one lucky baby, ma'am. She couldn't have found a better home," Sheriff Dawson said adamantly.

That afternoon, the Lapp family climbed into the buggy and rode two miles west of their farm. When they past the intersection, Emma said, "It is hard to fix my mind on thinking about this being the spot where Annie was shot."

Her father replied, "If you think it is hard for us, think what it will be like for Jonah and Freda from now on. We have to do our best to help them understand we forgive Jonah."

Jonah came out of the barn. When he recognized them, he came slowly to meet them. He bowed his head and trudged with slumped shoulders. Freda came out on the front porch. She folded her arms around her waist and walked toward them.

Jonah greeted, "It is gute to see all of you. I do not reckon you would like to come in?"

"We would be pleased to have you visit awhile if you wanted to," Freda said timidly.

"That would be gute," John replied. "Jonah, we wanted to see if we can get you to dress our fryers when you have time."

Jonah's eyes filled with tears. "Are you sure you want me to do that? Have you heard what I did?" He asked remorsefully.

"The sheriff told us this morning," Hal said, reaching down by Jonah's side to take his trembling hand.

"And still you would grace my home?" He asked in disbelief.

"Jah, we understand how this terrible accident happened to our Annie. Jonah, she would not want you to suffer from this. We do not want you to suffer," John explained.

"Still I will. This will haunt me the rest of my days," Jonah said, his voice full of remorse. "I'm so sorry that I was so careless."

John said, "We wish somehow to make this easier for you, Jonah. Let us come in and talk awhile."

"Before we leave, can you give us a date to come butcher the fryers so we know you are coming? Freda can come with you. Emma and I will have a gute dinner for you," Hal said.

"Jah, I will," Jonah replied as they went up the porch steps.

Chapter 17

Fall was in the nippy air late that afternoon. Hal snuggled her sweater up around her as she came through the mud room door with a pail of eggs. Where had the summer gone?

Placing each egg in the crock bowl on the table made her think about watching Annie do that chore. How things had changed in the last few months for the Lapp family. Bishop Bontrager was right when he said life did go on.

After the crazy, scary summer and losing their Annie, the days at the Lapp farm passed with enough to keep them all busy to take the edge off their grieving.

Jonah and Freda had come for the day a few weeks ago while Jonah dressed fryers for them. Emma was going to school with Noah and Daniel and really enjoyed teaching. John and the other farmers had started harvest now. Hal had her hands full trying to take care of two babies and the Lapp home. There were days she missed Emma being in charge. She even thought wistfully about what it would have been like if Annie was still around to help her. Then she remembered, by now Annie would be married Bobby Keim and moved to his house. Hal was on her own now and doing quite well if she did say so herself. Although, she kept reminding herself it was a learn as she went process.

She almost dropped the last egg when she heard from out front, the angry voice of a man yelled, "Get away from me!"

Hal rushed to the living room window and pulled the white half curtain aside. A buggy had parked in front of the clinic. She found it harder to hear a horse and buggy sometimes than a car. It seemed odd to think that, but she was getting used to the sound of horse hooves and wheels so she didn't always notice one going by. When company appeared out of the blue and caught her unaware, she missed Patches, their dog. He would have barked a warning.

She watched the farmer's brown beard flopped back and forth to the second button on his blue shirt as he rushed to the porch. Not far behind him raced Tom with his wings out spread. The man raised his hand to knock on the door as he looked back over his shoulder.

Hal opened the door. "Wilkcum."

Without introduction, he burst past her. "Close that door quick. There is a mean turkey after me."

"Sorry about that. Tom has been really disagreeable lately," Hal apologized.

"He bit me on the leg," the man said, rubbing his right calf. "No time to stand around. You and me have to get going." He opened the door and peeked outside. "That turkey is not in sight. Let's go." He grabbed Hal's arm, pulled her onto the front porch and went down the steps two at a time. Hal had all she could do to keep from falling. "I need you to come with me. It is too far to go to Wickenburg. There is no time. The delivery time is now, and she's having trouble. I need help right away."

"All right, but stop right there!" The man hesitated at her sharp voice. "I've got to bring my nursing bag and two babies. There isn't anyone else home to watch them."

Hal wrenched her elbow out of his grasp and rushed back into the clinic. She was the only one home that day, and she didn't know how long she would be gone. Babies took awhile to come into the world. As per John's orders, she jotted a note that she was going with a farmer to deliver a baby. She didn't know how long it would take or who he was. Beth and Redbird were with her. She left the note on the kitchen table where Emma would find it when she got home from school.

By the time Hal grabbed her green bag and bundled up the babies, the farmer was pacing along side his buggy. She placed both baby in one cradle. It was a tight fit, but she didn't know what else to do.

"We can take my car if we need to hurry," Hal offered.

"Nah," he said, standing on one foot and then the other.

"It's all right to use my car for medical emergencies. The bishop said so," Hal assured him.

"I know this, but you maybe can come with me this time for this medical emergency in my buggy," the farmer insisted, frowning at the babies. Redbird gurgled and Beth smiled at him. The man looked as if he didn't want to be bothered with a babies which seemd particular to Hal. The man was just about to become a father. Was he going to make that face at his own baby? He assured her, "I will bring you home later."

"All right. I didn't catch your name," she said.

"I am Rudy Briskey." He stepped up into the buggy. "Climb in. We do not have a minute more to waste."

Hal lifted the cradle up to him. "Take the cradle and put it in back on the floor." She climbed in and shut her door. Rudy clicked to his horse, whacked the horse's back with the lines and pulled on one line so that the horse turned in a tight circle to head back out the driveway.

Hal tilted to the side as the enclosed buggy went into a creaky lean. Redbird chortled as Hal straightened back up, and then Beth laughed. Hal tried to keep her mind on the delivery as she asked, "How long since her labor started?"

"Not sure. Found her that way awhile ago. Watched her for awhile. Saw I needed help." He clicked to the horse and snapped the lines over the animal's back to pick up speed as they left the driveway.

Hal stiffened her body and held on to the seat tight with both hands, thinking the constant rocking motion might make her sick at her stomach. "If you think she's having trouble, you maybe should have a doctor look at her."

"I thought you have delivered babies," he said, nodding behind him.

"Jah, but there are some obstetric problems that need taken care of by a doctor," she explained as she listened to the buggy moan when it shifted on its frame.

The farmer studied Hal's delicate, tender hands. "Take too long to get to town. I think you can handle it." As an after thought, he said, "Your hands are small enough."

Hal frowned. She didn't know what her having small hands had to do with delivering his wife's baby. Maybe this man didn't know much about delivering a baby, but she didn't have any intention of going in after the infant.

Rudy whipped the horse to a fast run. Hal hit her head on the buggy top when they bounced in and out a pothole. "Ouch!" She hissed. Redbird whimpered at the sound of her mother's sharp voice. Beth squeaked.

It occurred to Hal that she didn't know if there was a speed limit for buggies, but if there was Rudy was certainly exceeding it. She wished she hadn't had to bring the babies with her. This ride was not a safe one. "Does this buggy have a slow moving sign on the back of it?"

"Jah, why you ask?"

"I was wondering if it fell off." The hint went right over the man's head. Have you ever been a buggy that fell apart?"

"Not that I remember. Don't you think this buggy is put together all right?" He asked.

"I hear a lot of moaning and groaning under my feet," Hal worried.

"That's normal on the rough roads. Do not think a think of it," He reassured her.

As many times as she had taken a ride in their buggy, she'd never heard it protest like this one. Maybe she should concentrate on the patient to keep her mind off how fast they were going. "Is this her first pregnancy?"

"Ach, nah. Nancy has had others." Rudy shook the lines against his horse's back to speed him up more.

Hal felt the breeze from the open window spiking her hair out away from her face. Hopefully, if the woman had other births, this one wouldn't be as bad as the farmer thought. "How many?"

"How many what?" The farmer asked.

Hal knew she had to be patient with the man. His worried mind was on his poor wife and what was happening at his house while he was gone. She asked quietly, "How many pregnancies has she had?"

Rudy thought about that a moment. "Can't remember. Six or seven."

"You can't remember how many?" Hal looked away to keep Rudy from seeing her displeasure. Plain people had big families, but how could he lose count about something as important as how many times his wife had been pregnant?

"Nah, but she usually always has twins. I can tell you that. Maybe she's having triplets this time, and that is the problem. She is getting older you know." He looked at Hal as if she should understand what age had to do with a multiple birth pregnancy as he flicked the lines on the horse's back to sped him up again.

As the buggy took a sudden surge forward, Hal threw her hand out to grip the front of the buggy to keep from pitching ahead and out of the seat. "She usually has twins? How many babies has she had?"

"Do not know. Been long enough so that I have lost count," Rudy said, watching the road ahead.

How could a man have children running around him inside and outside the house and not know how many he fathered? The more she heard, the more Hal wondered if she could handle this delivery. It sounded too complicated. One that she wasn't schooled for. "If this will be a multiple birth, I think you really should think about getting the doctor. At the very least,

183

do you have a midwife around close that could come help?"

"Ach, nah, I already stopped at Edna Mast's house down the road. I tried to talk her into helping me. She refused," Rudy said, sadness in his voice that she treated him that way. "You were my last hope."

Hal was inclined to side with the farmer on this one. "That's awful that she turned you down when you needed help." The thought crossed her mind if Edna Mast had consented to go with Rudy she wouldn't be on this roller coaster ride with her two babies.

"I was thinking myself it was not too kind of Edna, but it is not for me to judge her." Rudy gave Hal a dejected look as he said, "You were my last choice." He turned into the drive.

"I see," Hal said quietly, but she felt like snapping back with thanks alot. She wondered if Edna Mast knew something about this delivery that she didn't. What could she be getting herself into?

The farmer pulled into the driveway and parked by the barn. Hal checked on the babies before she stepped down. Thank goodness for small blessings. They had dozed off. Rudy hopped out and tied the horse to a brass ring attached to the barn wall. When he turned around Hal was headed for the house.

He protested, "Nah, Nancy is not in the house. My wife wouldn't stand for that. Nancy is in the barn."

"She's having her babies in the barn!"

Rudy looked puzzled. "Jah, that is where she always has them."

Oh, this is all so wrong on so many levels, Hal thought. This farmer and his wife needed some lessons on cleanliness and sterilization. This must have been the reason Edna Mast said she wouldn't help.

The farmer ushered Hal toward a straw laden pen. She searched the pen over. There wasn't a woman in it. Mrs. Briskey must have come to her senses. She escaped and took to her bed in the house before Rudy got back home. Hal eyed the noisy female sheep in the pen. Standing in the far corner, the very bloated ewe, grunted, hunched up and gave Hal a pain filled look with her big dark eyes.

"Poor Nancy. She has not delivered yet. It is like I thought. She does need help right away," the farmer said in distress.

Hal stared at the man. Suddenly it dawned on her, Rudy Briskey and she had been having two very different mental pictures of one conversation about a maternity delivery. "You want me to deliver *her* babies?" Hal pointed a very stiff finger at the ewe.

"Jah." It was as simple as that as far as Rudy was concerned.

Hal had come this far of her own free will. She could see he certainly didn't expect her to back out now as he opened the gate and pushed her ahead of him into the pen. "She has to be in trouble to take this long." He looked off into space while he explained Nancy's possible problem. "You see when there is more than one baby all their legs get tangled up sometimes. The lambs need separated on the inside of her, but my hands are too big. Your ain't. You can stick your small hand right in there easy like."

"Like I said before. I don't have schooling for a difficult birthing. I really think you should go after the veterinarian," Hal protested.

"Ach, nah. No time for that as long as she has been in labor. You are here. You will do just fine. I know you will. You are a nurse. You know these things," he said with a confidence that Hal didn't feel.

The farmer seemed so sure Hal was the answer. At least that is what he would have her believe. She didn't want to make him angry at her, but this task, in her opinion, was beyond the call of a nurse's duty to her patients. On the other hand, Stella Strutt was enough in the Plain community to have after her hide at one time. The woman had been stilled for awhile, but who knew what might set her off. Something as simple as refusing to deliver lambs for Rudy Briskey might do it. If Rudy told the story of her refusal, he'd be sure to mention her along

185

with Edna Mast as two very uncaring females. Stella would take delight in hearing Rudy's description of her.

She walked around behind the ewe, wondering how she could possibly do what this farmer was asking of her. Bloody strings dangled down from the opening, oozing out along with one small pink hoof. Human babies usually came out on their own. She hadn't figured she'd have to go in after them. That was a job for a doctor or in this case a veterinarian. Hal looked at her hands and winced when she thought of going inside that unhygienic ewe to pull her lambs into the world.

Hal said resignedly, "You wouldn't have some gloves I could use I suppose."

"You want to put on gloves?" Rudy looked as if she was asking for the moon.

She shrugged her shoulders. "It was a thought or maybe not."

He reached behind him to his back pocket and held out a pair of cotton yellow chores gloves to her. Along with them, he admonished, "If you intend to wear these I might as well try to put my big hand in there."

No use trying to explain she wanted sterilized gloves. "I see what you mean. It was a bad idea. Never mind. How about bringing me some water to wash in."

He looked at her outstretched hands. "You want to wash up before you pull the lambs." He sounded like that was the craziest thing he'd ever heard.

It ran through Hal's head that if he only knew, she had had much crazier thoughts in the last half hour than he could ever come up with. "My nursing training has taught me that I need to have germ free hands to do a delivery. We don't want the mother to get an infection from my hands being dirty. Could you just humor me, Randy?"

"My name is Rudy." The farmer corrected as he raced for the barn door. Clearly, he felt that Hal was wasting precious time. From the way the bloated ewe hunched up and bawled in misery, the poor creature might be thinking the same thing.

"Rudy, check on my babies to see if they are still sleeping, Hal ordered as he slammed the bottom barn door.

He twisted around. "Mind if I take the cradle into my wife to watch?"

"That's a good idea, Rudy. Do that for me."

She looked around the barn, feeling panic set in. Should she find a back door to escape from? She might be able to walk half way home before the farmer came back and found her missing. No, that wouldn't work now that the babies were in the house.

In a few minutes, Rudy came through the door with a pail of warm water, sloshing out of the pail and down his trouser leg. He had a towel draped over his arm. He set the pail in the pen and held onto the towel.

He didn't bring a bar of soap. She wanted to mention that little detail but decided it might not be a good idea. Not after he started to pace like an expectant father, having a hard time waiting for her to get to work. She took off her sweater and tossed it over the side of the pen. Next she rolled up her long sleeves so she could wash her hands. She surveyed the laboring ewe and rolled her sleeve on her right arm way up past her elbow. No telling how far she'd have to stick her hand into that ewe. The farmer handed her the towel. She dried, and draped it over the pen. Taking a long, deep breath, she said, "I'm ready. Hold the sheep still for me, please."

The farmer got a good grip on the ewe's neck and braced his feet.

On the back side, Hal sank to her knees in the straw. Beneath her knees, smelly amniotic fluid soak into her dress from the soaked straw. She chose to ignore that. Not that she liked the warm, sticky wetness and knowing what it was one little bit, but she knew she had a lot worse ahead of her. She closed her eyes and ran her hand in along side the tiny hoof and went as far back as she could. What she felt was hot and sticky and all legs.

The ewe strained at the foreign object inserted in her to rid

187

herself of it. The tightness numbed Hal's arm. She held her breath, bit her bottom lip and waited for the mother to relax. She felt around and managed to figure out what the farmer had tried to explain to her about tangled legs. She did a mental map about which back legs belonged to the lamb in front. She was able to unfold the other front leg from under the first lamb's body, trying to even it up with the hoof sticking out of the opening. She pulled on the legs. They grew more exposed along side her grimy arm. The ewe strained and the lamb's head popped out. The tiny body slid down onto the straw. Along with the lamb came a rush of fluid that landed in Hal's lap before she could move out of the way.

"You did it, Nurse Hal," Rudy praised.

She looked cryptically at her dress. "It seems I did."

Rudy studied the lamb closely. "Just what I thought. That lamb is too small."

"That is not my fault. You want me to put it back," snapped Hal.

"You are a joker, ain't? Go back in and see if you can help the others," he ordered.

With more room inside the ewe to work, Hal had an easier time on the next go around making out the legs of another lamb. She pulled and gently brought the lamb out into the world with the ewe's pushing contraction. By that time, the first baby was crying and sneezing the fluid out of his nose, making a red mucus stripe along the side of her green skirt. The ewe, tired of being held, twisted her back end one way then the other, trying to get out of the farmer's grip. She wanted to tend to her bawling babies.

Hal wiped her forehead with the top of her sleeve to get rid of some splatters. "Are we done now?" Rudy got a better stance and took a tighter grip around the ewe's neck. "Hold on. Not yet. Check and see if she's done, Nurse Hal."

"Done?"

"She might have one more lamb in there," Rudy said hopefully.

Per Rudy's instructions and with more confidence now, Hal put her hand back in that ever widening opening one more time. She felt two more legs way back inside, grabbed hold and tugged. At the opening, she realized the tail was with the legs, not the head. "This lamb is backward."

Rudy's voice sounded alarmed. "Just keep pulling quick. It should be all right if it hasn't been inside for too long."

The lamb slid out. Hal laid it gently on the straw. "It's not breathing, Rudy." She watched with dread, fearing the lamb was dead.

The farmer turned loose of the ewe. He snatched up a piece of straw, stuck the end in the lamb's nose and wiggled it around. The lamb flinched. His nose wrinkled up. He sneezed and his sides moved with thumpy movements.

"You did it. He's breathing. That was a neat trick," Hal said excitedly.

By then, the second lamb was shaking his head convulsively, trying to make sense of this new world and what he was supposed to do next. The first lamb was struggling to stand up. He made it to his feet unsteadily and staggered back to his knees, but he knew he had to keep trying to stay on his feet if he was to walk and eat. The lamb sensed dinner was close by. The frantic mother licked first one then the other, trying to figure out which needed the most care first. A muffled rumble hummed from deep in her throat that was a comforting sound to the babies.

The first lamb edged stiff legged along the ewe's side. He nosed his mother's bag and stuck his small pink tongue out to lick around, searching for a teat.

Hal was amazed. "How does he know where to go?"

"Nature, Nurse Hal. The babies are born knowing where to go right away. Once they pick a side, the mother will never let them change places. She will turn around in circles until the babies are in the right place or make them start over. Nature is a voonderball gute thing when we have babies on the farm," Rudy declared.

189

"These lambs are so cute." She bent to touch the last one born. The ewe gave a warning stamp of her foot and nudged Hal's hand away with her nose. Hal backed out of the way. "Does that mean she doesn't want me to touch her babies?"

"Jah, it does so it might be better to get out of here. We need to get some more warm water. Now is when you should wash up," Rudy suggested as if he needed to teach her.

Hal chose to ignore his reference to her hand washing. "I think it would be fun to have sheep. Do you enjoy taking care of them, Rudy?"

"I do. I expect I owe you something for your services. I have a couple ewes I could give you to get you started if you would like to have a flock. I could even load them up and bring them along when I take you home."

"Really. Oh, this is great. My very own sheep. Oh, but you don't have to pay me," she protested.

"Jah, I think I should. If not for you, I would not have three healthy lambs."

"Denki, so much," Hal said.

When Hal burst into the house, John came up out of his rocker and ran across the room to meet her. "Emma, come quick. Hal, what has happened to you?"

Emma and the boys came from the kitchen. Emma said, "Hallie, you're bleeding. How bad are you hurt?"

"I'm not hurt at all." Hal set the cradle down, thankful that the babies hadn't woke up yet. She looked down at her dress and brushed at the clinging straws. Wasn't much she could do for the dried stains from the ewe's after birth but soak and wash. "I guess I do look a mess."

John came closer to inspect her. "With all that has happened lately, we thought you were in danger." He sniffed. "Smells like you have been in a barn. Where have you been?"

"Your note just said you were going to deliver a baby," Emma said.

"Who in the district is due right now?" John asked Emma.

"No one that I know about. You did say in the note you were

190

going to deliver a baby, Hallie," Emma repeated.

"I did do that. Three of them in fact," Hal boasted.

"Ach, nah! What woman had triplets?" John asked.

"No woman had a baby. Now listen to me all of you. Give me time to explain, but John, next time you go to the salebarn I want to go along. I'd like to buy some sheep if you don't mind"

"Sheep. You want sheep?"

"I just helped Rudy Briskey deliver triplet lambs. It was so much fun. Well, maybe not all of it was but watching those cute little lambs was fun. I think the boys will enjoy helping me with a flock of sheep. In fact, Rudy Briskey gave me two mothers to start my flock with for my payment. He unloaded them into a pen in the barn. Want to see?"

"Jah, I think we all do," John said. "One thing, Hal. No one is supposed to have to pay you for what you do for them."

"I didn't ask for payment, and I told him that. Rudy offered. Actually, he practically insisted," Hal assured him as she went in the barn door.

"Knowing Rudy, that is what bothers me," John said as they looked over the pen wall at the two thick wooled sheep contentedly munching on a block of hay.

Hal beamed proudly at all two of her new flock.

John slowly shook his head and frowned.

"This is the wrong time of year for lambing. That is in the spring," Noah said.

"Not when Rudy Briskey does it. He lambs twice a year so he has some lambs coming in the fall," John said.

Noah looked at the sheep skeptically. "Daed, do you think Rudy give Mama Hal two bucks?"

"Why would he want to do that?" Hal asked.

Ignoring her, John surmised to Noah, "Can not tell with all that wool. Knowing Rudy Briskey, he would give her wethers instead of bucks."

"Rudy told me these two are mothers and are going to have lambs soon," Hal insisted.

Daniel cheeped to Noah and John, "Look and see,

191

somebody."

"Gute idea. Noah, hold them for me." John and Noah climbed over the pen. Noah caught one then the other while John examined under their bellies. "These are both ewes."

"See just like Mr. Briskey said," Hal said, brightening up.

"I would not get my hopes up if I was you, Hal. I think these two ewes days of being mothers are gone," John surmised.

"How can you know that?"

"First of all, they have not been sheared for awhile. That tells me Rudy did not think he wanted to bother with them so he did not shear the wool off. The ewes have mastitis in their bag which is -----."

Hal interrupted shortly, "I know what that is. I grew up around dairy cattle. Remember?"

"The ewes are worth something for slaughter. I'll take them to the salebarn. In the spring, we'll look for some that would make a more promising flock if you still want sheep by then. There is no sense in feeding these ewes all winter. How does that sound?"

"But Rudy said these sheep would have lambs soon," protested Hal. "I want to wait until they lamb."

Noah looked doubtful. "I do not think you should trust Rudy. I can not see him giving anyone a bargain. It is not in his nature. There has to be something we are missing."

"It will be awhile before I can go to the salebarn We can wait that long," John said to appease Hal.

A couple weeks later, each ewe was the mother of two babies. Hal and Daniel were in the pen with the new families, feeding the lambs from pop bottles with little black nipples attached. John and Noah came from the milk parlor to watch.

"You having fun yet?" John asked, trying to suppress a grin.

"Sure we are," Hal said. "Aren't these the cutest babies you ever saw?"

Noah snorted, "Daed, now we know what was wrong with Rudy's bargain. This was too much work for him. He did not want to have to feed the lambs on the bottle."

192

About the Author

Fay Risner lives with her husband on a central Iowa acreage along with their sheep, milk goats, chickens, rabbits and cats. She has one son, Duane. A former Certified Nurse Aide at the Keystone Nursing Care Center in Keystone, Iowa, she now divides her time between writing books, working in her flower beds and the garden and going fishing with her husband in their boat.

Fay has an online bookstore at www.booksbyfaybookstore.weebly.com and an author site at www.writersownwords.com/booksbyfay. Both sites have her blog posts if you want to keep up with the author.

Fay Risner uses large print in her books to make them reader friendly. Her books have a mid western, Iowa and small town flavor. She pulls the readers into her stories, making it hard to put a book down until the reader sees how the story ends. Readers say the characters are fun to get to know and often humorous. The books leave the reader wanting a sequel or a series so they can read about the characters again.